C000225379

Bound from England ⬚⬚⬚⬚⬚⬚⬚⬚⬚
bean in 1670 to marry ⬚⬚⬚⬚⬚⬚⬚⬚⬚
into the hands of the n⬚⬚⬚⬚⬚⬚⬚⬚⬚
Venn, known to his ac⬚⬚⬚⬚⬚⬚⬚⬚
just cause to hate all ⬚⬚⬚⬚⬚⬚⬚⬚
reason to fear for l⬚⬚⬚⬚⬚⬚⬚
jealousy of his mistress, who sails the seas as the Rav⬚⬚
lieutenant and sees in the lovely Joanna a deadly rival,
does nothing to allay her fears.

Her strict upbringing tells Joanna she must resist the
Raven's desires. Yet, terrifying as this voyage is, when
he offers to release her to join her fiancé as planned, she
asks herself if this is what she really wants?

By the same author in Masquerade

DUEL OF LOVE
CHANCE OF LOVE

Sea-Raven's Bride
Helen May

MILLS & BOON LIMITED
London · Sydney · Toronto

First published in Great Britain 1981
by Mills & Boon Limited, 15–16 Brook's Mews,
London W1A 1DR

© Helen May 1981

Australian copyright 1981
Philippine copyright 1981

ISBN 0 263 73755 1

The text of this publication or any part thereof may not be
reproduced or transmitted in any form or by any means,
electronic or mechanical, including photocopying, re-
cording, storage in an information retrieval system, or
otherwise, without the written permission of the
publisher.

This book is sold subject to the condition that it shall not,
by way of trade or otherwise, be lent, resold, hired out or
otherwise circulated without the prior consent of the
publisher in any form of binding or cover other than that
in which it is published and without a similar condition
including this condition being imposed on the subsequent
purchaser.

Set in 10 on 11pt. Times by

Rowland Phototypesetting Ltd.,
Bury St Edmunds, Suffolk
Made and printed in Great Britain by
Cox & Wyman Ltd., Reading

CHAPTER
ONE

JOANNA crouched in the hot, nauseous cabin, clinging to
a bulkhead rail, fighting the queasiness induced both by
the heaving seas and her filthy surroundings, and prayed
that the ship would founder and end her misery.

Empty bottles rolled with every motion of the waves,
releasing the odour of stale wine, while discarded food
rotted slowly in the heat.

Soiled garments thrown down among the quantities of
rich materials were an unpleasant contrast to the
brocades and silks, velvets and satins; jewels and ornaments of magnificence and cost were scattered
haphazardly about.

Joanna's head drooped lower and her long white fingers clutched and writhed as she listened to the sound of
crashing timbers from above decks and the drunken
oaths and yells.

She was shaken with horror at her fleeting wish that
the men would die in the storm when all the teaching of
her faith proclaimed mercy and forgiveness. Yet would
the men and women who had preached such a doctrine
during the many hours she had spent of her eighteen
years in quiet parlours still propound their gentle
philosophy if they had been forced to witness the violation and murder of women who had been her kind and
dignified maids, and the destruction of the honest seamen who had sailed the merchant ship to the waters of
the Caribbean?

She would never now arrive at New Providence Island
in the Bahamas where her betrothed awaited her. Her
head swam and she felt ill, remembering her panic as she
had knelt on the deck of the little merchant vessel,
praying incoherently. One of the brutal pirates had

seized her and the man who commanded them had struck out with his cutlass, sending her assailant sheering off with a curse.

If Joanna had hoped for mercy she was disappointed. Her rescuer had roared, 'This beauty's mine!' and she shuddered at the thought of him. He was big with fat and muscle, greasy skinned, tangled haired, unwashed, teeth broken and stained, and in the instant he had held her against him she had been repelled by his rancid breath.

He had dragged her below and locked her in this cabin and now she wished she had perished with her maids. She would have known brief agony, quick shame, then merciful death; instead she must wait the arrival of a man who filled her with utter repugnance and dread and who would prolong his pleasure.

Before he left her he had swept off his feathered hat and rendered an awkward bow. 'Cap'n Pryce, at your service. Buccaneer and owner of this ship and now of you!' And with a coarse laugh he had gone.

The ship's timbers groaned as the wind-driven waves tossed the helpless vessel, battering her with destructive force, and as the wind rose to a howl it seemed as if the ship's back must surely break.

Then with incredible rapidity the storm died and was followed by a silence which seemed unnatural. Had all the men been washed overboard? Her heart thudded as she heard movement and shouts and soon there came the sound of clumsy footsteps, the door was unlocked and Captain Pryce was framed there, red-eyed and leering. If he had gone to his Maker during the storm he would have arrived very drunk.

He slammed the door shut behind him and advanced with outstretched hands and moist mouth and Joanna backed away until she could move no more and pressed herself against the bulkhead, closing her eyes in despair.

'Sail ho!'

The cry halted the pirate and he swore, then took a step nearer. The door burst open and a crewman yelled, 'It's *him*! It's the Raven!' He began to babble. 'You promised us he'd gone off to America. You said we'd be well away by the time he got back! Now he's seen us and he's crowding on sail. He'll be on us in minutes and we're helpless.'

'Not quite!' bawled Pryce. He looked round at Joanna, 'I'll be back, sweetheart.' Then he leapt for the companionway, leaving her locked in again.

She had never had experience of battle, but there was no mistaking the noise of gunfire and the whistle and crash as the attacking gunners found their target. The already weakened vessel staggered like a drunken sailor and smoke began to drift beneath the cabin door. Joanna coughed and her eyes smarted. Her horror increased. If the ship burnt she was sure that her merciless captors would not give their prisoner a second thought.

The sounds of battle faded and the smoke increased and she pounded on the door. Running footsteps passed and repassed the cabin and at last someone let her out. She held up her skirts and scrambled above decks where she saw flames had taken hold on rigging and a coil of tarred rope. Grappling irons linked the vessel to a sleek brigantine whose name was painted in large gold letters—*Lady Margaret*. The decks were slippery with blood which mingled with water from the leather buckets with which men were fighting the fire.

A large blond man who had arrived with the *Lady Margaret* was pointing out to sea and she saw a boat in which Captain Pryce and some of his men were rowing hard. 'Shall we follow them, sir?'

A voice commanded him to leave them. 'Recover the treasure in case we lose the ship.'

Men scurried about carrying chests and sacks, bolts of cloth and containers of precious oils and spices and Joanna, who seemed to be forgotten in the turmoil, went

as far as possible from the fire to stand among a group of
men she recognised as members of the crew of the
merchant ship from which she had been captured.

'How many of you survived?' she asked eagerly. 'Are
any of the women safe?'

One of the men shook his head. 'Not one,' he said
sadly, 'and only we are left of the men. The murdering
swine holed the ship and drowned some of the crew.'

Joannas's eyes pricked with tears and her throat ached
as all hope for her maids died. Standing apart there was a
smaller group of men who were gaunt and filthy, their
once fine garments stained and torn.

The seaman nodded at them. 'Spaniards. They were
in the hold.'

Joanna heard them talking in their own tongue and
caught one word which sounded vaguely familiar. '*Pi-
ratas*!' They gesticulated to the men carrying the treasure
aboard the *Lady Margaret*.

Joanna said, 'They talk of pirates, I think. Are they
discussing Captain Pryce and his crew?'

The seaman turned a look of despair to her and she
knew the answer before he spoke. 'We're just as bad off,
Mistress Seldon. They're scurvy pirates, every one.'

Joanna watched her new captors. She had been unwilling to admit to herself that they were no ordinary seamen, but their gaudy raiment, their coloured scarves and
gold earrings, the mixture of races and insolent, speculative glances sent her way confirmed the truth of the
seaman's words.

The fire was controlled and the big blond man called
instructions before walking towards her with determined tread while a slender red-haired youth cried
gleefully, 'Go on, get the Spanish bitch!'

Joanna turned and grasped the deck rail, hauling herself up. She would take her chance over the side, but she
was grasped from behind and dragged back and set on
her feet with a spine-jarring thump.

She stared into the face of her tormentor who was not, as she had expected, the blond man. He was hurrying away, glancing back at her with a resentful look, fingering a blackening eye.

The red-haired youth swore. 'Why stop him from taking his pleasure? Not going soft are you?'

The man ignored him and stared at Joanna. He was about thirty, burned brown by the sun; black hair brushed his enormous shoulders, dark eyes, deep set, burned into hers.

His voice surprised her. It was low and modulated. 'No Spanish woman this! Her dark gown and pure white collar are Puritan's holy raiment.'

The words were spat at her and Joanna shrank from the vituperation in his tone. Yet, not only had he spoken in English, but he was cultured. Surely such a man would not harm her even if, for some inexplicable reason, he loathed her. She tried to speak, but repeated shocks had frozen her tongue, then the dark man seized her about her waist and lifted her without effort. He shouted to the *Lady Margaret* for attention and tossed her across the water into the grasp of one of his men.

She was set on her feet, the world spun round and she slid into oblivion. She regained consciousness to find herself where she had fallen. The shouts had stopped and she raised her head.

'You feeling better, mistress?'

The incongruity of both words and accent brought her near hysteria. 'You are a West Country man,' she breathed.

His face broke into a smile, 'That's right, born and bred in Somerset.'

He was of medium build, thin and tanned with pale blue eyes. He had a curiously honest air in view of his calling. She thought with nostalgia of her home so far from these burning decks, of the green fields and shady lanes, of her scholarly father working quietly in his bookroom. He was a man of modest estate, opposed to the creed of His Majesty King Charles the Second, and had betrothed her, at fifteen, to a man of like beliefs. Matthias had sailed for the Indies two years before in search of freedom and prosperity and her father had watched her set sail with confidence in her future.

The man was watching her sympathetically, his eyes enquiring and she said, 'I also am from the west—I was born and reared in Devon.'

'I never went there, but I'm told it's lovely. Will Buckley's my name. What's yours?'

'Joanna Seldon. I did not know that Englishmen like you could be pirates. Somehow I always thought of them as evil foreigners.'

His good humour was unimpaired. 'There's bad men in all races, mistress, but we're not pirates. We're privateers. Some call us buccaneers.'

He actually sounded proud and Joanna asked bitterly, 'What difference is there? It seems to me that the murdering and robbing are the same!'

'No, mistress, you're wrong. We attack only the king's enemies. The Spaniards are our game.'

She licked her dry lips and Will proffered a flask. ' 'Tis good wine.'

She wet her parched tongue and swallowed a little. 'The men you have just attacked were not Spanish.'

His teeth were bared in a grin. 'That they weren't. Cap'n Pryce and his evil crew should have known better than to steal a ship and treasure from a servant of the Raven. Now Pryce—he's a real bad pirate—he'd sell his own mother.'

'The man who threw me on board—he is the Raven?'

Will nodded and Joanna sipped the wine, wishing it were the clear, sweet water running from the Devon hills. On the voyage out the water had soon grown brackish and the ale sour, but she felt she would have preferred even them to wine which did not quench her thirst. She stirred restlessly, trying to bring ventilation to her damp skin. In her mohair gown she was unbearably hot. When Matthias had written of the heat she and her father had pictured the brief warmth of an English summer day. She had been ill prepared for the relentless sun, even with the tempering of the prevailing breezes.

Will spoke again. 'The Raven don't allow killing except of enemies and in defence. We always take prisoners when we can.'

Her eyes lit in quick hope. 'To release?'

He laughed. 'If they're Britons, we let them go, unless they want to join us. The others—we sell.' His tone had grown grave and Joanna wondered if he had stomach for such transactions.

'Slaves!' she said disgustedly. 'But I am English! So will he let me go?'

Will avoided her eyes. 'You'd best ask him, mistress. It ain't up to me.'

Joanna barely had time to wonder what mercy she might expect from the black-haired devil who held her captive, before the Raven swung himself to the half deck and ordered Will to leave. The small man gave her an encouraging grin, before he touched his forehead and slithered down the gangway on bare feet which acted like another pair of hands.

Joanna scrambled to her feet. She found it difficult to remain still beneath the scrutiny of the dark eyes which seemed to pierce her brain. Sweat trickled inside her shift as she stared at him. His face was devoid of expression, his huge body, garbed in black with silver slashed sleeves and a scarlet cravat, was muscular, his hands were long, the fingers well shaped.

'I am told you were found in the main cabin—the one occupied by that thieving dog, Pryce.'

His implication was unmistakable and she flushed. 'I did not choose to be there.'

'How did you come into his possession?'

Joanna's blue eyes sparked fire. 'I was not his *possession*!'

He shot her a look of hate. 'How long have you been aboard his ship?'

'How long? I do not know exactly—a few hours.' Her voice was ragged.

'A few hours,' he repeated. 'And spent in the company of Pryce and you maintain that he has not taken your body?' Again the cruel eyes raked her. 'You are not unattractive.'

Her self control deserted her and she sprang towards him, hands flailing. 'Wicked! Beast! You enjoy torturing me!'

He caught her wrists in an iron grip and held her helplessly at a distance. Her shrieks drew the attention of men in the rigging, who hung there like bunches of gaudy, evil fruit, staring, their mouths stretched in lewd grins, while two climbed the companionway to peer. They were driven off by the Raven's snarled imprecations. His lips curved sensuously revealing strong teeth, white and even. Joanna saw that she amused him. She knew she should stop struggling. Yet his smile did not reach his eyes which remained icy.

For a few moments longer she tried to free herself, then her strength collapsed and she quivered, panting, in his hold.

Again the Raven allowed his eyes to travel over her. 'You still insist that Pryce had power over you for hours and left you unmolested? It is impossible!'

'There . . . there was no time. The storm blew up and then you came.'

'Delivered from the wolves to my hounds, eh?'

He spoke almost musingly and Joanna said, her voice breaking in a way she despised. 'Please, release my hands.'

'I do not want my eyes scratched out. Either you behave or I'll have you put in irons.'

She swallowed hard. 'I will not struggle.'

He let her go and keeping her voice even and full of reason she told him why she was at sea and where she was trying to go. 'So you see, sir, you would be performing an act of charity if you delivered me unscathed to my betrothed. You are an English gentleman . . .'

'You are mistaken, madam! I am a privateer and owe nothing to any man or woman, save my shipmates and the gentleman who holds my commission.'

'For the sake of the gentleman you once were . . .'

To her horror his teeth showed in a grin. 'What I have become is my *only* reality, and nothing else!'

Her mouth was dry. 'Sir, I have not deserved a base fate.'

The dark face grew darker with fury. 'How many deserve what life sends?'

She replied gently, 'How can punishing me help anyone else?'

At the look in his eyes she almost recoiled. 'Damnation on you! Keep your tongue still or you may stir up a demon.'

She had sensed a compulsive anguish and pursued, 'My faith teaches me to offer comfort wherever possible . . .'

'Your faith!' he sneered. 'You are a Puritan?'

'I am, sir.'

His grin was more like a snarl. 'Puritan.' He made it sound like a servant of the devil. 'A ranting, canting Puritan. Well, you stay aboard my ship!'

'Have you no pity?'

'For such as you? None whatsoever!'

'What . . . what do you intend to do with me?'

Her tongue flicked her lips nervously as he stared at her, his heavy black brows drawn together in a scowl. Then his mouth twisted. 'The possibilities will make interesting speculation for you, madam!'

The red-haired youth climbed to the halfdeck. 'The

flames are quenched. We can hoist enough sail to bring her to port.'

'Good. You will command her. Take what men you need.'

The youth's full lips were sulky. 'I prefer to sail with you.'

The Raven did not raise his voice. 'You will obey me or receive a lesson on who is master.'

The youth shot Joanna a look of such intense hatred she caught her breath, then he returned to the other ship, shouting orders.

The Raven jerked his head towards the companion-way and Joanna tried to descend, but in her confusion she stumbled, caught her slender foot in her heavy hem, and almost tumbled. Her captor gave an impatient ex-clamation, picked her up and carried her to the deck where he set her on her feet carelessly.

The men who watched called advice both specific and lewd, bringing the shamed blood to her face, before they swarmed aloft to unfurl the sails and when Joanna raised her eyes to watch she saw the buccaneer's flag for the first time. A raven, coal black against a white ground.

'It is a carrion bird,' she exclaimed scornfully.

The captain turned his sardonic gaze on her. 'You are right, madam! A fitting symbol for one who has vowed to destroy scum.'

They took a leisurely course to allow the damaged ship to keep pace. Joanna was not confined and had opportunity to look about her. She was surprised at the immaculate cleanliness everywhere. She might have been aboard a merchantman or even a naval vessel. The difference lay in the excessive numbers of men who were needed when the fighting began. They had no particular tasks and lay or walked everywhere, looking at her with lascivious eyes and moist mouths and she was glad when at last the Raven led her into the main cabin set above decks.

The small paned windows relieved the sun's glare and she blinked in the dimness. The cabin was furnished as sparsely as her father's bookroom. Here also were plain oak chairs and chests and drapes of dark blue. She was invited to take a place at a carved table where Will brought chicken and wine and she broke her fast for the first time for many hours.

Afterwards the Raven rose and removed his coat. Her heart pounded. Was this the start of her violation? He seemed calm and when he turned to her with a grin she saw that he had exactly gauged her mind.

'I am hot,' he said laconically.

Will arrived, his arms filled with clean garments, and the captain went into an inner cabin and appeared moments later in a long black velvet coat.

He bowed to Joanna, 'I wear this in respect for your Puritan modesty,' and she knew that beneath it he was naked.

She waited, her heartbeats suffocating, but he went outside and she realised that men were lowering pails to the ocean and drenching him in sea water. He returned, his bare feet leaving small pools on the deck which Buckley wiped before going in to his master. Again she waited, expecting every moment to be summoned, knowing that outside only worse could befall her. She felt ready to collapse from strain when her tormentor came out wearing a fresh suit of black cloth, the ruffles at his wrists as snowy as his neck cloth. The only colour lay in the ruby set in gold on his right hand.

'You may use the small cabin for your toilet,' he said.

Joanna shrank back. 'No!' She was terrified at the idea of removing her garments while this huge muscular devil was so close.

'I will leave Buckley on guard,' he grinned and she knew that once more he had read her mind correctly and she flushed.

'I . . . I will cleanse myself later.'

'You will do it now! When I held you the heat from your person was enough to burn me. The Caribbean holds dangers for one newly come from Britain. Cleanliness is a precaution against disease.'

'Are you a physician as well as a murderous pirate?' she flashed.

There was complete stillness for a moment then he replied, 'I will tell you now, madam, and I do not wish to repeat myself, that I am not a pirate. I am a privateer and hold a commission from His Majesty's governor of Jamaica. Only the enemies of our people need fear me.'

'That is not so,' she retorted. 'A Puritan maid should also fear you!'

She waited for an explosion of rage, half hoped for it since it would give her further chance of argument in favour of her freedom. He simply raised his hand and pointed to the inner cabin door. 'Inside, madam, and disrobe.'

At her beginnings of protest his face darkened. 'Either you remove that crow gown or I do it for you.' He took a step towards her and she rose and ran into the cabin, terrified, scorning herself for allowing him to know. He was a vile bully, she stormed. She pulled at the black mohair and stood in her shift, the relief of air on her skin momentarily swamping all other feeling, then a rustle at the door made her grab her gown and hold it to herself.

Will Buckley appeared holding a pail of water, his eyes averted. 'Don't be afeared, mistress, I'll not shame you.'

He placed the water by the door and held out his hand, 'Cap'n says I'm to take your gown.'

Joanna smothered a sob in her throat. Before she could speak Will said, 'Best do as he says.'

He twitched a shawl of many-hued Indian cotton from a chest and Joanna pulled it about her before allowing the man to remove her gown. Then she resigned herself to the inevitable and stripped down to her white skin. The water was like a caress after the hours of stifling confinement and as she laved and dried herself in the rough towel provided she could hear the soft movements of the Raven in the adjoining cabinet.

There was a tap on her door and she dragged the shawl around her. Again Will entered and held out his hand. He said impassively, 'I've orders to take the rest of your things, mistress.'

As Joanna protested he stared ahead and she was defeated by her embarrassment and his impervious attitude. She turned aside and muttered to him to take them away.

When she looked back she discovered a neat pile of fresh garments. She picked them up and fingered them gently, holding them to her cheeks, feeling quick shame at her undeniable pleasure in the feel of silk and satin, the glowing colours. All her life she had been admonished by those who suspected that she wearied of plain white linen and dark wool. Her most frivolous gown had been grey for festive occasions. She had been disciplined, first by her mother before she died, then by her old nurse, when her craving for the soft, bright clothes worn by their enemies, the royalists, had spilled into speech, and she had dutifully tried to prefer her Puritan garb. She threw the silken garments down, anger coursing through her, unable to decide if it was at herself for her treacherous pleasure, or the hateful buccaneer who had forced her unwittingly to face the frivolous part of her nature.

A burst of coarse laughter from the deck sent her trembling back to the clothes. Even Luther himself would accept that a maid should wear any garments rather than remain naked in the power of such lewd captors. She pulled on the pink silken petticoat and shimmering blue satin gown, lacing her bodice with shaking fingers. She felt unbelievably free without the restriction of her whalebone stomacher which she had been taught to wear for modesty rather than need. Her figure was firm and slender. She found a silver comb, undoubtedly wrested from some grand lady, and used it on her softly waving golden hair which she twisted into a loose knot behind her neck. Automatically she looked for a kerchief for her bodice and colour flamed down to her gently swelling breasts when she realised that for the first time in her life she was expected to appear before men with so much white skin glowingly visible.

Footsteps approached the door and she grabbed the shawl, wrapping it round her shoulders and bosom. There was a knock and the Raven entered, his tall, wide-shouldered form making the cabin shrink. She felt, rather than saw, his dark eyes encompassing her appearance. Once she dared to raise her gaze and lowered it quickly at his sardonic humour as he saw the way she clutched her shawl.

To cover her embarrassment she snapped, 'I suppose you stole these things from some poor woman!'

He gave his humourless laugh. 'We appropriated them, certainly, but only from the chests in a Spanish treasure ship . . .'

'It is abominable that you, a man of education, should sink so low as to hurt and steal from defenceless women . . .'

'Do you, indeed, madam. Allow me to inform you that we removed the garments from a cargo which was to be used to bribe ignorant Indians into revealing more of their treasure, or for the harlots of the coastal towns. No Spanish woman of repute would wear them.'

As the implication of his words sank into her brain Joanna cried, 'And you think them suitable for me!'

'A virtuous woman should rise above her circumstances.'

The words of Puritan teaching fell incongruously from lips curved in a mocking grin.

'Why do you take such a delight in tormenting me? What have I done to deserve it? Those men out there are little better than animals, but you . . .'

She gasped as he grasped her wrist cruelly. 'Those men out there are my brothers, madam, so have a care.'

Rebellion rose in her throat so violent that she tasted it. 'Brothers? Thieves! Murderers! Violators of women . . .'

The Raven threw back his head in a shout of harsh mirth. 'They give as they have received. They do what has been done to them and their women.'

'And is that what drives you on?'

Joanna had felt above fear in her angry indignation, but she shook inside now at his expression. His voice was soft and terrifying. 'What drives me on, madam, is my affair. Let me assure you that this life is the only one which could ever satisfy me.'

She fell silent before such malignant hate and he dropped her wrist. It ached from the cruel pressure of his fingers, but she dared not move to rub it. The cabin was permeated by some dark emotion which was suffocating in its intensity.

Then her tormentor said, 'You have told me you are Joanna Seldon on your way to New Providence. What awaits you there?'

'My betrothed, Master Matthias Kemp. He sailed three years ago to make a new and free life for us.'

'It is to be hoped he is a strong man for these islands are no place for a weakling.'

'He is an *honest* man, sir.'

The buccaneer simply stared at her and she said, 'You are the Raven, are you not?'

He swept her a mocking bow. 'Kester Venn, at your service.'

Somehow he seemed to assume normality with a name. The nightmare horror faded a little and she said,

'I beg of you, Master Venn, will you consider taking me to my future husband?'

'Is he also a Puritan?'

'Of course! To what other manner of man would my father send me?'

'I fear he will have to remain disappointed.' The Raven laughed and the sound was ugly. 'And I have a title, Sir Christopher Venn, but you, my pretty Puritan, may call me Kester. And I shall address you as Joanna. How friendly we shall be.'

CHAPTER
TWO

JOANNA stared. 'You were born to high estate and you roam these seas as a vagabond? I wonder that you do not give your talents to your own land.'

'My land! My gracious monarch repaid the sacrifices made for the royal family by granting what was left of our estates to a royalist who shared his exile.'

'Surely if you returned to claim them . . .!'

'There is little left to claim. Our manor was destroyed by the upstart Cromwell. My work people were starving and needed a man with money to give them employment. I would not go to them as a beggar. Now too many years have gone by—it is all too late.'

'It is iniquitous. You should petition the king.'

'Do you think he would view my cause with justice? You amaze me! I would not have expected a Puritan maid to defend His Majesty. We have something in common, after all.'

Joanna was abashed by his mockery. She said hesitantly, 'Are your parents living somewhere here?'

She took a small step back before the cold fury in his face. 'Enough prying questions, madam!'

'I had not thought of prying. I was intrigued by your title.'

'When you have been longer in the Caribbean nothing will surprise you. It is peopled by those whose stories are more amazing than mine.'

She seemed about to argue and he threw her a frown. She subsided as Will entered. 'Take this, mistress, you'll need it.'

She stared at the hat he held out to her. It was of blue

cloth with a row of tiny silk daisies round the brim and a large curling plume.

'I am accustomed to a simple cap and hood,' protested Joanna.

Kester seized the hat and rammed it on her head, pulling and twisting it until it sat to his satisfaction. 'You will wear it. I want no sick woman on board my ship.'

Joanna gave way. She had found the heat oppressive and since reaching tropical waters had spent the hotter part of the day in her cabin. Now Kester Venn opened the door and she stepped out on to the deck. The buc- caneers sprawled everywhere, more than needed to sail the brigantine, but not too many to raid Spanish ship- ping. All hands were needed then to pursue their bloody calling, Joanna reflected contemptuously. She tried to ignore the glances sent her way, but their eyes pursued her, hot and lascivious as they encompassed her softly swelling form in its revealing gown, and she felt fresh indignation at the man who had removed the shawl from her shoulders.

A remark by a pock-marked man caused her to draw to the side of the Raven who shot the man a warning glare from between narrowed lids. The man repeated the remark and the captain's arm shot out. He ducked, but was too late to avoid his master's anger and reeled back, blood flecking his mouth.

Joanna's heart beat hard. There could be trouble and she was afraid. What if something happened to Kester Venn? He terrified her, but not so much as the men who watched her like cats thirsting after a bowl of cream. But the man subsided, a half grin on his ugly face, as his comrades sneered at him. They were like a pack of wolves only barely controlled by a master who was more savage than they.

He kept her by his side as they patrolled the ship and she realised that this was his way of parading her before

them as his woman—his possession. Her sudden awareness sent waves of burning humiliation through her,
followed by revulsion. Was she destined to be his woman
in truth? She passed the remaining hours of daylight in
an agony of trepidation and when the tropic sun descended with its usual suddenness behind the horizon,
leaving the sky a bowl of brilliant stars, she entered the
main cabin, her breathing ragged and uneven.

Kester motioned her to a table where he joined her
and they ate meat, fruit and bread which he washed
down with long draughts of wine. She tried to conceal
her qualms and eat normally, but she could swallow only
with difficulty. He kept his gaze on her, a mocking smile
curving his mouth, his eyes cool and hard. She was on
the point of begging him to leave her alone, but she
hesitated to speak. So far he had not harmed her. Why
reveal her suspicion? Surely it would be better to act as if
she expected absolute courtesy from him.

When he made an abrupt movement all her resolution
crumpled and she shrank back. He reached into the fruit
bowl for a peach and she knew by his face that he had
read her mind exactly and was amusing himself.

He poured a generous measure of wine for her and
when she shook her head he frowned. 'Drink,' he ordered. 'Your body needs moisture and we cannot give
you water until we take on fresh supplies.'

Beneath his arrogant stare she lifted the glass and
drank and the wine flowed down her throat, making her
feel both weak and more confident at the same time. It
was fruit flavoured and pleasant and she sipped again,
then drank deeply. It was far stronger than she realised
and it was with horror that she felt her command of her
faculties sliding. She was tired too. Tired and anguished
by the events which had overtaken her. She would give
much for a bed into which she could sink and sleep and
forget everything. But she sat opposite this devil in his
cabin, the flickering lamp sending shadows over his face,

deepening his eyes, making his grin into a mask of mocking torment.

She half rose then fell back into her chair, staring at him, her blue eyes wide and anguished in her pale face. He touched her cheek gently with a long brown finger. 'How beautiful you are,' he murmured, half to himself. 'You skin is so white and pure. It is many years since I saw a complexion like it—softened by the moisture of an English climate.'

Terrified of antagonising him Joanna stayed still though his touch seemed to burn her. Dear God, how long would he torture her? At any moment he was going to force her into the inner cabin where the huge four-poster bed was bolted to the floor.

When he rose suddenly she almost screamed. He bowed. 'Come, madam, you look exhausted. Time you were abed.'

Stupefied by wine and fear Joanna dragged herself across the cabin. At the door she gave him an imploring look and he smiled. He threw the door open and stood back. 'Pleasant dreams, Puritan maiden.'

She looked into the dark eyes, unable to speak, and he said, 'Afraid, Joanna? You may sleep in a chaste bed tonight.'

With a sob she sped through the door and it shut behind her. She waited, staring at the small lamp which swung from the ceiling. Then she opened it, blew out the light and, with shaking hands, pulled off her gown. She crept into bed in her shift and stockings feeling somehow safer than if she had stripped. She heard Will Buckley enter the other cabin, the murmur of voices, then silence. She lay frozen in the dark, then Kester's voice came to her, 'Good night, mistress. I shall be here all night so do not hesitate to sleep. No one will molest you.'

Against all reason she believed him and she was extremely weary. She fell asleep in the midst of her prayers.

The weather continued calm and the ships made slow progress. Joanna was permitted on deck only beneath the watch of the captain or Will whom he appeared to trust implicitly. She could not quarrel with his caution. The men lounged, watching her, their mouths moist with the frustration of idle time at sea.

Some played cards and once a quarrel broke out between a big German and a Nubian. Knives were drawn and Joanna believed it inevitable that one or both would die and the spotless decks be stained with gore. But Kester Venn appeared almost silently and the knives were sheathed and the game continued. A man produced a fiddle and another a Moorish guitar and some of the buccaneers sang with surprising harmony. For a while Joanna viewed them as seamen thrown together by circumstance, rough fellows, but goodnatured, until one caught her eye and a murmured remark sent them into loud laughter which brought the blood to her cheeks.

Kester's voice said close to her ear, 'My sea dogs are difficult to hold in leash, madam.' His voice was grim, his face hard, and Joanna bit back a retort. He was as unpredictable as his men and she had no wish to provoke a scene to amuse these evil creatures.

Once he ordered Joanna to remain in the main cabin with Will seated cross-legged before the door, a musket in his arms, loaded and cocked.

'He has orders to kill the first man who approaches the cabin,' said the captain as calmly as if he were conducting a child's game. 'I shall be on the other ship for an hour or two. Do not attempt to go on deck. I need scarce remind you what will happen if my dogs get out of hand. A woman's honour is not something which can be restored.'

Any reply she might have made was lost in the sudden savage fury in his tone. She shrank back, made abruptly aware as she was so many times each day of his barely

controlled malignity towards her. She watched through
the window as the oars of a small boat rose and dipped,
sending dancing ripples over the calm ocean. She saw
him swing himself aboard to be greeted with a smile by
his red-haired lieutenant, then she sat and awaited his
return, her heart thumping uncomfortably. She loathed
and detested him, but she could not deny she felt safer
when he was present. Safe, that was, from other men.
She had no way of knowing his intention for her. Sometimes he seemed to regard her with scalding contempt; at
others she could swear she saw a flicker of . . . of what?
She dared not pursue such thoughts further and began to
roam the cabin, opening and closing chests and
cupboards, scarcely knowing what she did. She glanced
briefly at the neatly folded piles of fresh linen and outer
garments in their sombre colours and fine lace. Her
attention was riveted by the contents of a small leather
chest.

Books! She seized them in unbelieving joy. Who
would have supposed a privateer to read? She knelt at
the chest, arms deep inside, lost for a while to danger.
There were ballads and plays by men whose names were
anathema to her father for their lewdness and she
blushed and put them aside. Her fingers found a Bible
and she renewed in the familiar words a sense of peace
and consolation. She looked at the flyleaf and saw
names. His parents and several brothers and sisters.
Against each was the same single date written in heavy
black strokes. Joanna supposed that some dreadful
plague, or maybe a disaster, had carried them off. Was
that why he was bitter? But many families were destroyed
by disease. It was unavoidable. It must be accepted. His
mother's name had been Margaret; the brigantine must
be named after her. The edges of the pages were singed
and flaky. This Bible had been through fire.

She placed it down reverently and picked up a volume
by Donne, and assuming it to be a book of sermons,

opened it. When she saw the love poems she was assailed by curiosity and began to read. Time halted as the sensuous words brought to her veins a tingle of something which eluded her understanding, but which gave her yearnings of terrible intensity. Perhaps her father was right when he warned her that she was a woman of unruly longings which must be curbed.

She was still on her knees reading, her soul gleaning joy from the glory of the poetry, when the door was thrown open and the captain strode in. As always he seemed to fill the cabin. She shut her book quickly and he looked down at her, then he was bending over her, gripping her wrist.

'I see you have made free with my personal belongings, madam!'

'As you did with mine!' flashed Joanna, before she thought.

He released her hand, but stood too close, his body towering above her, aggressive in its masculine nearness. He took the Bible and stared at it with an unfathomable expression. 'So, Miss Puritan, you have discovered your life guide.'

Joanna saw her conduct through his eyes. 'I . . . I should not have pried,' she stammered. 'I was desperate for something with which to occupy my mind.'

He was almost gentle. 'I had not considered the matter, but of course, I should have done. It must be obvious that a woman of your quality could read. It has been a long time since I was close to such a one. You may use the books.'

He approached her and removed the Donne poetry book from her hand. 'John Donne, by all that's holy!' He threw back his head and laughed and all gentleness had vanished, leaving his manner ugly. 'So! Puritan ladies read love poetry, do they?'

Joanna said quietly, 'I . . . I am not always a good Puritan. My father has often chastised me.'

He grinned. 'Has he, indeed? To little effect, it would seem. I begin to view you in a different light.'

Joanna's flush stained her white skin. 'Reading a book does not make me bad.'

'I did not suggest it.' He seemed to lose interest, stretching his arms above his head and yawning. He appeared relaxed and she was surprised, assuming him to have been engaged in consultation with his fiery lieutenant.

The remainder of the voyage was uneventful. She walked the decks, or read, and the two ships dropped anchor off the *Isle des Vaches* on a warm, glowing evening which filled Joanna with a strange aching longing.

Kester came to her where she stood staring at the island and she said, 'Oh, please may I go ashore? It is weeks since my feet touched land.'

'You will remain on board, madam!'

She opened her mouth to fling a furious protest at him then stopped as his face darkened. For a moment she had forgotten she was his prisoner to deal with as he chose.

He bowed slightly, 'I am here to conduct you below decks.'

Her eyes widened and she said, 'Please, do not shut me away! I cannot bear to be imprisoned. If I give my word to obey you will you allow me the freedom of your quarters?'

His lips tightened. 'I am accustomed to obedience and I desire you to go below.'

Still she hesitated. She had allowed the peace of the ocean to envelop her. They had seen sails in the distance once or twice but Kester had disregarded advice from his men to pursue other prey. 'They are greedy,' he told Joanna. 'The holds of the ship are laden with riches and they would risk all for more.'

Joanna had looked at him amazed. He could label

men greedy, yet his life seemed devoted to acquiring gold. She had held her tongue. He had been treating her with consummate courtesy and she found it pleasant. In her state of euphoria she was able to keep the murder of her maids in the back of her mind, still too numbing and fresh to be examined. Kester Venn had not killed them. Will said he hesitated to kill.

She moved to the companionway. 'Do you mean to put me with the other prisoners? Am I to be sold as a—slave?'

His frown daunted her. 'Go below,' he said harshly. 'It is not for you to question me!'

A prickle of fear ran up her spine. What a fool she was to allow herself to be lulled by him. He was the bloodthirsty buccaneer she had first believed. She climbed down steep ladders to the shadows below and was surprised and relieved when the captain threw open a door to a tiny cabin.

Someone looked up as they entered and for a moment Joanna was held in breathless astonishment. A woman in a shimmering green gown stood there. She was burned gold by the sun and her eyes, even in the dimness of the cabin, glowed large and brown. She threw a derisive grin at Joanna who was convinced that somewhere they had met before. The small head was crowned by red-gold hair which flowed down over the slender shoulders and with a shock Joanna recognised the woman as the red-haired lieutenant.

The implication of what she was seeing was like a blow. The woman said softly, 'Yes, we are acquainted. And now *you* will occupy this cabin while I join my lord in my rightful place by his side.'

'Have done!' Kester growled.

The woman did not take her eyes from Joanna's pale face. 'You look shocked, Miss Puritan! Did you think that Captain Venn had no place in his life for softer human needs?'

'Will you have done, I say? Must I give you a lesson in obedience?'

The woman sank a deep curtsey. 'It would be a pleasure to learn from you any time,' she mocked.

Kester turned and strode away and the woman said, all smiles gone, no warmth left in her sibilant voice, 'I will kill any woman who tries to take him from me!'

She took a step nearer, thrusting her face into Joanna's. 'My friends aboard this vessel tell me that your eyes have followed him with something more than curiosity. Keep a watch on yourself. No one takes what belongs to Claris Talbot.'

She slipped through the door, locking it behind her, leaving Joanna to sink on to a small chest and stare at the bulkhead in the imperfect light from a small lantern. A moment passed during which suffocating panic in the tiny windowless enclosure brought breathlessness and tingling nerves. She took deep breaths, dragging composure about herself like a cloak. She must not give way. No doubt it would afford amusement to her captors to find her clawing hysterically at the door. She clenched her sweat-drenched hands, remembering Claris Talbot's face, wondering why her discovery hurt so much. Why not? she told herself. Any Puritan maiden confronted by a harlot and her loathsome protector would be outraged. Now she had seen Claris in woman's dress she pondered her previous blindness. The girl was beautiful and, in spite of her bloodthirsty calling, retained an incredible quality of girlish attraction. Her voice held a country burr and Joanna guessed her to be the daughter of a farmer or a tradesman. What had brought her to the Caribbean as a privateer's woman? Was Joanna destined to end as the bed-mate of such a one as the Raven?

She sprang to her feet and walked round and round, struggling with the certainty that there could be no other man like Kester Venn, stifling the suspicion that if he wanted her she would find resistance difficult. What was happening to the innocent, virtuous girl who had set sail to be wed? She brought her betrothed's face to mind, recalling when they had last met and what her feelings had been when she was informed that she was to be his bride.

The saturnine features of the Raven blotted out her promised husband and she sat down heavily, a sob escaping her. Unbidden came the picture of Claris Talbot in the great cabin with Kester Venn. The four-poster in which Joanna had lain through the soft Caribbean nights while he guarded her in the day cabin would be occupied by them. Dear God! She must halt such wanton imaginings.

The door opened abruptly and she looked up, hoping that the Raven repented her imprisonment. She could scarcely hide her disappointment to see the homely features of Will Buckley. He handed her a pile of books.

'Cap'n's compliments,' he muttered.

He left quickly, but she saw that his face had contained a measure of sympathy and chagrin.

Joanna placed the books on a chest. She could not read. She could not rest. She found her writhing fingers had torn the lace at her breast. A thought made her face burn. Perhaps she was actually wearing one of that woman's gowns. She looked in the chest and saw folded clothes. Gowns of green and crimson, blue and gold, shawls, slippers, a black lace mantilla. Not one was quiet or reserved.

The door opened once more to admit Will with food she picked at. Then she drank a draught of wine, undressed and climbed into a wooden bunk and tried to sleep. The long, restless night gave her plenty of time to brood on her situation. She dozed fitfully and when she awoke found the perpetually damp, below-decks cabin had taken its toll. Her head ached and she had an unpleasant taste in her mouth, and when she tried to stand her head throbbed and she turned giddy. She dressed and sat down to wait. Will arrived with a plate of steaming fish and she turned her head, her hand on her mouth.

He put the fish down. 'Are you sick, mistress?'

She nodded, gagging at the smell of the food and he removed it. He brought back a man she had not met before. The stranger was thin and his eyes were bloodshot, he swayed and spoke in a thick voice. His coughs racked his bony frame, but cleared his speech.

'Are you ill?' His tone was genteel and he sounded kind and she found it difficult to hold back sudden tears.

'Who are you?'

'The ship's surgeon and physician.' At her astonished look he smiled thinly. 'Oh, yes, mistress, even buccaneers need physic and after battles there is much work to be done. Some of them may even destroy priests, but medical men are always spared.'

'Are you a prisoner also?'

His voice rasped an answer. 'Yes! But not of Captain Venn. Now, mistress, what ails you?'

Joanna explained and he held her wrist and laid a hand on her forehead. The answers to his questions made him nod. 'I shall speak to the Raven. It is obvious what makes you ill.'

She was not left alone for long. Within moments Kester arrived, his white shirt unbuttoned to the waist, revealing his muscular neck and the strong dark hairs which grew thickly on his chest. Joanna, after one irresistible look, turned her head away.

He gave a low laugh. 'I forgot your Puritan modesty. I do apologise.'

He was mocking her and she remained silent. 'I have spoken to our surgeon,' he said, 'and he assures me that your incarceration in these rather odorous quarters has made you ill. I am here to invite you back to my cabin.'

Joanna stared at him. The idea of going back above decks brought a surge of fresh nausea. Presumably it meant sharing with his harlot, condoning their relation-

ship. A thought struck her with anguish she found bewildering. 'Are you wed to that red-haired female?'

His black brows formed a ridge over his angry eyes.
'What has that to do with you? Oh, I think I understand!
You do not wish to sully yourself by coming into contact
with Claris unless we have had the blessing of the
church!' His harsh bark of a laugh jolted through the tiny
cabin. 'I should leave you here to stew, but I will not.
You will accompany me to the main cabin!'

Instantly Joanna became set in her determination to
oppose him. 'I will remain here where the air may be
poor, but is chaste!'

He took a step towards her and once more his
masculine presence loomed too close, too invasively
dominating. She moved back until her legs came up
against a locker. He followed her, reaching for her. A
hoarse cry of protest rose before he seized her arms in his
merciless hands and his mouth descended on hers. His
kiss bore no resemblance to the hesitant salute offered
her by her betrothed. It seemed to drink her senses from
her, to drain all powers of resistance, until she stood
helpless and trembling before him. When he removed
his mouth there was an instant during which he looked
startled. He released her arms and stepped back. Joanna's eyes blazed hatred. She longed to strike his
arrogant face, to bring blood seeping from scratches, but
she held still. He had absolute dominance over her and if
she provoked him he could easily take from her the final
bastion of her maidenhood.

He brushed a hand over his mouth before he laughed
shortly. 'Come with me, madam,' he commanded, and
this time she did not refuse. At the very least he could lift
her and carry her to the upper decks where she would
provoke more of the lewd remarks and coarse laughter
of his men.

She stumbled after him, struggling to thrust down her
innate honesty which was forcing her to admit that her

question about whether or not he was wedded to Claris
had not been prompted by any conventional modesty,
and that his kiss, forced upon her though it had been,
had continued to foster the idea that she was jealous of
Claris.

She entered the day cabin to find its austere neatness
destroyed. Feminine garments lay on benches, a
hairbrush had been dropped and left to lie, a pair of kid
slippers and something made of frothy lace were
abandoned across the partly opened door to the inner
cabin. Joanna's cheeks burned and Kester grinned, kicking the brush so that it slid across the deck and into the
door.

'Come get your things, slut,' he called good-
humouredly.

Claris Talbot pushed open the door and leaned on the
jamb, pulling her disarranged robe of yellow silk about
her. She gave her lord a brilliant smile before she saw
Joanna and instantly her face was transformed to fury.

'What is that woman doing here?'

'These quarters are mine!' Kester's answer was brut-
ally brief and Claris's brown eyes narrowed and the blood
ran up under her skin. Joanna felt sorry for her in that
moment and made the mistake of allowing her pity to
show. She thought Claris would leap at her and kill her.
The passions in the cabin were almost tangible and
Joanna wanted to shrink back, pleading for a truce. For
the first time in her life she was being made to face the
searing flames of base desires and she felt she could not
endure such dominant and perpetual hostility. She took
a ragged breath and from somewhere deep within her
spirit she drew an inner strength. She said nothing, made
no move, but something about her apparent tranquillity
seeped through to Claris whose temper subsided. She
strutted about, muttering in a sullen fashion, as she
picked up her possessions before disappearing through
the door.

Joanna sank into the only comfortable chair on board and Kester poured her a glass of wine which he handed her. His twisted grin told her that he recognised her triumph over his mistress.

'No wine,' she begged, shaking her head. 'It would make me ill.'

His voice was calm. 'This is the juice of Caribbean fruit,' he said.

'Why cannot I have water?'

He continued to hold the glass to her and Joanna felt unutterably weary at the idea of another clash. She took the glass and tasted and was surprised by the combination of previously unknown flavours. The drink was cool and she sipped gratefully. The fresh air was already taking effect and by the time she had finished her drink the malaise had gone.

Later the three of them broke their fast, sitting together at the table. Claris lost no opportunity in making it apparent that Kester Venn was her man. He appeared to regard her with the indulgence he would afford a kitten. Joanna kept her eyes on her plate. The food was well cooked by Will Buckley who seemed to hold it his life's work to minister to his master's comfort, and Joanna ate fish and small sweet bananas, washing her meal down with more fruit juice. Afterwards Kester and Claris, who changed into her male attire, left the cabin and Will cleared away. Joanna was alone again and everything was as before. No, not quite. For now she knew of the existence of Claris Talbot. She walked restlessly about the cabin, wondering why a brazen buccaneer's woman should have the power to disturb her so. Once she glanced into the inner cabin at the bed which had not yet been smoothed and gorge rose in her throat. She told herself that disgust with their lecherous behaviour was paramount.

Yet when she was joined by the surgeon she was driven again to ask, 'Are they married?'

He sat down and turned his thin, haggard face to her. 'Not to my knowledge,' he answered, 'though much happens about me that I do not comprehend.'

Joanna seated herself opposite him. 'You are ill, sir. That devil has made you wretched.'

'No!' He was vehement. 'I was past hope before I was carried off by Captain Venn.' He smiled. 'He was my salvation in many ways. The evil demon of drink has brought me to misery. I bungled the treatment of a nobleman and might have lost my life. I escaped on board a merchantman and was captured by Kester Venn. He offered me a position as surgeon. In truth I had no choice in more ways than one. I have been with him four years.'

He peered closely at her. 'You seek to know more of him. Pray, do not. Such a man is not for a gentlewoman like yourself.'

Blood flamed in her face. 'I care nothing for him! I seek only to allay my . . . my boredom.'

'Is that so? Well, take care you do not meddle. His patience is not long and he is unused to continence in any form and you are a very beautiful woman. My age, my profession, allows me to say so. Beware of these sea-dogs. They are not men such as you are used to.'

'I am only too aware of that,' retorted Joanna bitterly.

She told him of the fate of her maids and the others who had been on the outgoing vessel with her. As she spoke the numbness dissolved and the terrible scenes came vividly alive. Her tears flowed and she sobbed in helpless grief and despair. 'Wicked, evil men!' she stormed. 'And your precious leader is no better than they!'

'Many would tell you that the Raven is to be infinitely preferred to Captain Pryce, or indeed, to any buccaneer who sails these waters. He at least was born a gentleman and retains much of his inner breeding, though he strives to forget it at times.'

'What makes him so bitter?'

The surgeon looked at her with his lack-lustre eyes. Then he shrugged. 'Anyone could tell you his story. It is quite common. His family was driven from England by Cromwell in 1653. They settled on one of the islands and endured terrible privation. The Indians were hostile and their crops were destroyed repeatedly. Kester's mother was not strong and his father no farmer. Kester, at thirteen, was the eldest of numerous progeny and there were more babies, most of whom perished at birth.'

Joanna swallowed hard. 'I found a Bible. One date lay against the names of his family. Was there a plague?'

The man's laugh reminded her of Kester in its harshness. 'Aye, you might say so. A human plague. Spaniards landed on the island to replenish their supplies. They amused themselves with Kester's family. He returned from a hunting trip with their manservant to find his home on fire and his family all dead, or dying. He held his mother in his arms as she died and she, poor weak soul, spared him nothing of the details of the ravishment of herself and his sisters.'

Again there was silence and Joanna breathed. 'Puritans and Spaniards! He hates them all for what they did to his family!'

'That he does. He blames them equally for their destruction and the loss of his birthright.'

Joanna wanted to know more, but the door opened and Kester Venn's large body blocked out the light.

'We are going ashore, mistress. Do you want to come?'

'Oh, please.'

She found the wide hat and her shawl and in a moment was climbing down into a boat manned by some of the less disreputable seamen. Other boats were laden and there was an air of festivity.

Joanna wondered why only a skeleton crew was left aboard until she saw the chests and boxes being stowed on the white sandy beach. The buccaneers were about to divide their spoils.

Sickness choked her. Was she to be part of it? Had she been tricked to come peacefully to shore by soft words? She looked up and saw Kester Venn's eyes on her. They were hard and filled with mockery. Was he now about to revenge himself on the Puritans who had begun the annihilation of his family?

CHAPTER
THREE

As the men pulled into the narrow channel leading to the *Isle des Vaches* it became clear why Joanna had not been offered water. The small island was barren and windswept and boasted almost no vegetation. A place without attractions and perfect for dividing treasure since the men would have nothing else on their minds.

Joanna climbed ashore, assisted by Will, and walked where he pointed, seating herself on a wooden spar, evidence of some long ago wreck. She strove to appear calm though her heart was thudding hard with terror.

The chests were dragged to a centre spot on the shore and she watched, mesmerised, as the quartermaster directed men to set out their contents. Gold and silver goblets, chalices and plate were heaped in one place; jewelled ornaments and boxes in another; rings, necklaces and brooches, earrings and coronets in a third heap of glittering value. Boxes were opened to reveal thousands of gold and silver coins from every country in the world; perfumes and unguents, silks, satins and brocades were separated and gradually the men who ringed the beach fell silent, their eyes eager, their mouths working with greed as the full wonder of their latest raids on Spanish galleons was revealed.

Then the sharing began and again the quartermaster took charge, ordering men whose aspect seemed less savage to assist. Kester Venn leaned on a tree, his arms folded, watching the proceedings impassively. Pistols were thrust into the wide leather belt at his hips and a sword was girded at his waist. Once there was a noisy disagreement which was referred to him.

He spoke softly, 'The man is right, quartermaster. His wound entitles him to more. He has lost three fingers, not two.'

There was no further argument and Joanna was amazed to realise that all who had been hurt in recent fighting received an amount commensurate with their injuries. A man with a patch where his eye had been took his extra hundred pieces of eight, another with a bandaged stump at the end of his left arm received five hundred pieces of eight on top of his ordinary share and one who limped along on one leg and a crutch shoved an equal amount into his canvas bag. He stumped back to his place amid rude jests which indicated that although his fighting days were over he might take any number of lives in his new position as ship's cook.

Will Buckley went forward and received his own reward and took charge of the captain's, and the surgeon, carpenter and other ship's officers received their due amounts.

Then Joanna saw something which turned her legs to jelly. More boats were being beached and the captives were led ashore. They were manacled and pale from their sojourn in the bows of the ship. She realised that Spaniards only were to be auctioned. The merchantmen evidently were to be set free. She was bitter to realise that her womanhood, which should have been her chief protection, was going to be responsible for further terror. One by one the wretched captives were paraded before the men who bid for them with as little emotion as they would have bid for cattle. Small, weaker men fetched little, but the strong brought good prices, one large fellow going for four hundred pieces of eight. The money made was divided equally, and everyone was stowing away his particular share when a clear voice spoke up. 'What of the woman prisoner?'

Claris Talbot, standing astride like a man, her bag slung over one shoulder, was staring at her. There were murmurs among the crew and Joanna saw that they were in agreement with Claris. She was part of a prize and as such was available to all.

The entire proceedings had been so calmly conducted that, if it had not been for the hopeless faces of the Spaniards now being led back to the boats in irons, Joanna could have mistaken the sale for an ordinary market. Now, suddenly, she felt exposed and terrified. How would Kester Venn react? He might have no choice in the matter. Already, one or two of the bolder men were sidling towards her and she saw the naked desire in their eyes.

Kester spoke evenly, 'The woman is not for sale.'

An angry muttering ran through the ranks of men and he continued, 'We will await a ransom for her.'

Joanna had difficulty in suppressing a gasp at the lie. She had never hidden the fact that her family had no money to save her. What were his intentions? Was he keeping her for himself. She had no time to ponder.

Claris was not easily set down. 'You've started ransom proceedings, have you?'

'Do not be absurd,' grated Kester. 'You know full well that we have not been near a town since we took her.'

Claris bit her lip, then said, 'The talk is that the woman has no money for ransom. She said as much to Will Buckley.'

Hundreds of eyes were on Will who did not flinch. 'You're mistook, Claris Talbot. You never heard such a tale from me.'

A ripple of anger ran through the company and for an instant the brightness of their turbans and shirts swam into a variegated mass before Joanna's eyes. If they chose to rebel what could one or two men do against them?

Kester had not moved nor taken his eyes from her. He said in an unemotional voice, 'If any among you desires to challenge my right to lead let him step forward now and we will settle it with a fight to the death.'

There was a brief silence during which men looked around uneasily. Someone made a joke, several rose and began to walk towards the sea; the crisis was over.

Claris went red with rage. Kester walked to her and her brown eyes filled with terror. He spoke to her in low tones and passed on, calling over his shoulder to Will to take Joanna to the boats. She followed him, passing close to Claris whose hatred seemed to seep through her skin to envelop Joanna in a grey mantle.

On board the brigantine Joanna was ordered into the inner cabin from where she heard part of a bitter altercation between the Raven and his woman. He ordered her to resume command of the damaged ship; she argued that the short voyage to Hispaniola could be conducted by another.

'Get that Puritan bitch below,' hissed Claris, 'or have you other plans for her?'

Joanna did not catch Kester's low reply, but she could not miss the lewd answer of Claris nor the shouts of mirth from the listening buccaneers.

Moments later she heard Claris angrily bidding men pull for the other ship and Kester entered the cabin and told her she was free to move about. She followed him into the day cabin where he pulled off his jacket and hat and poured wine which he drank before pouring more. Joanna waited for some word from him, but he simply began to busy himself examining charts. Finally he seated himself at the table and drawing parchment, ink and quills from a drawer, began to write.

Joanna's patience snapped. 'Have you no word for me?'

His eyebrows were eloquent. 'Of what should I speak, madam?'

'What do you intend to do with me? I have a right to know!'

He rose abruptly and strode to her, staring down at

her with his hard gaze. 'Aboard this ship you have no rights! You are my prisoner to do what I like with. Do not provoke me, or you will feel the weight of my anger.'

She struggled to control her voice. 'Cannot you show me mercy? Think of the anxiety of my betrothed—of my father when he learns of my disappearance—you once had a family . . .'

She stopped, petrified by the blaze of anger in his eyes. In her desperate attempt to make him see her point of view she had chosen entirely the wrong approach.

His voice contained venom. 'Aye, I once had a family. I suppose you have been gossiping with Robert Jennison, our worthy surgeon. Perhaps I should have taken out his tongue. He could practise his skills without speech.'

Joanna shrank back. She had been mistaken in supposing that the Raven's ferocity was a veneer over a civilised mind. Clearly he had forgotten any gentleness he might have known.

'I asked him who you were,' she admitted through stiff lips. 'He was not gossiping—he thinks well of you.'

'Does he, indeed? I care nothing for what he, or any man thinks of me, and least of all do I care for the opinion of a Puritan!'

'But I was not party to what happened,' burst out Joanna, driven on by her misery. 'I would never condone cruelty in any form to anyone!'

'And your family? Was your saintly family immune from the troubles in England?'

Joanna was silenced. Condemnation of the royalists and their ways had been familiar to her from her cradle.

'You cannot defend them, can you?' The Raven's eyes were coldly triumphant. 'They, as much as anyone, were responsible for what became of my family.'

'You were not the only one to suffer! The Civil War was a time of dreadfulness on all sides. If men continue to harbour resentments how will we ever live in peace? Each side was as bad as the other.'

His harsh tones struck her like a blow. 'I care nothing for the sufferings of others. I remember only the horror which came to me and mine!'

She opened her mouth for another argument, then gasped as he seized her arms in cruel hands. 'I wish to hear no more from you on the subject. One more word on matters which are not your concern and you will find yourself in the hold where you may fight the rats for food and bedding.'

He released her with a slight shove which sent her against the bulkhead and she hugged her arms in despair as he reseated himself and finished his writing without apparent emotion. His entire life was coloured by his boyhood experience and he was beyond redemption.

Shortly afterwards he went on deck, the men swarmed aloft, the sails were unfurled and the ship sailed. Their next harbour was off a shore very different from the *Isle des Vaches*. Trees grew thickly inland and Joanna heard the cries of many living creatures. Bright flashes of colour told her that birds were abundant and, high on a hill, she saw the sparkle of water where a spring bubbled out of the rock to cascade down to the sea.

She was assailed by a longing to walk in such a lovely place, to hold the sweetness of fresh, cool water in her mouth and let it trickle down her throat. She could not take her eyes from the sight and stared until her wish became a torment.

When Kester told her she was to go ashore she felt a leap of joy before sudden fear washed over her. Was another sale about to take place in which she would figure prominently? A glance at his unrelenting face made her understand that he gave her no choice and she climbed into a boat and was rowed ashore. Parties of men went inland to hunt and soon the huge cooking pots over wood fires were emitting savoury smells and bowls were heaped with unfamiliar fruit. Joanna enjoyed them, but still she yearned for the water. There was wine and ale in plenty doled out by the quartermaster, but there was no drunkenness. Kester Venn was everywhere, his dark eyes missing nothing.

The repairs to the fire-damaged ship proved simpler than expected, and the carpenter directed men to cut suitable trees and fashion the wood into the required shapes. Then, to Joanna's surprise, the brigantine was floated to the beach, her shallow draught making this easy, and ropes were fastened to her and men strained and heaved until she was careened.

Will Buckley explained that it was necessary to examine and repair the timbers often as they were liable to destruction by infiltration of teredo worms.

'The ships get slower and finally become unseaworthy. As you can imagine, mistress, it wouldn't do for us to be stuck with a vessel that couldn't outrun our enemies.'

'I wonder *you* live so precarious a life!' exclaimed Joanna. 'Surely a man like you would prefer an honest occupation.'

Will scratched his grey head. 'As to that, mistress, I don't know. I've tried most things early in life, including lawful seaman, and it's all terrible hard with no reward at the end. Now, with Captain Venn, we know we'll reap enough to keep us in our old age.'

'If you live to be old! It seems you risk your life overmuch.'

'Think you that the risks are less elsewhere? I tell you, mistress, I feel a good deal safer with the Raven than anyone. He's clever and a wondrous good seaman. Besides, I was with his family since I was young.'

Joanna stared. 'Are you the servant of whom the surgeon spoke? The one who survived the massacre?'

Will nodded, then had to leave as his master summoned him. Thereafter he was kept busy and Joanna watched the activities. Her stomach heaved as a breeze wafted the noxious stench of tallow, tar and sulphur from the calking pot. Kester Venn was nowhere in sight and Claris Talbot also was missing. She supposed they were together and her lip curled.

Suddenly she could not endure to remain still for another moment. No one was watching her and she strolled to the belt of trees which fringed the white sand. Expecting always to be hailed she found herself in their welcome shade and with a final short run she reached concealment. The undergrowth grew thick and she tore at trailing foliage, forced often to seek different ways, but she climbed steadily, the idea of the water now an obsession.

The trees and bushes thinned as she got higher and she went through sunny clearings where the heat struck back at her from rocky outcrops.

The sound of rushing water turned her aside and she pushed her way through a ring of thick shrubs and came upon a scene of infinite beauty. A waterfall dropped thirty feet into a pool before sending the stream on down the hill. Around the pool grew bright green bushes and brilliant flowers. One tree leaned over, its branches reflected in broken lines of green as the water flowed and bubbled. Joanna stared, enraptured, then gasped and a hand went to her mouth. At the water's edge appeared Kester Venn. He was naked and he raised his arms and dived, his tanned body cleaving a way through the clear water. Reaching the surface he tossed back his dark hair, sending out a crystal shower, and swam with lazy strokes to the centre of the pool where he lay on his back in the sun. Joanna had not realised she was moving until, with a shock, she found herself on the water's edge, her gaze caught by his.

He looked surprised, though not shocked, and for a moment, his guard lowered, she thought he seemed vulnerable, like the boy he once had been. Then the face set in the sardonic lines she knew and detested and he raised his arm in greeting. A quick flurry of water as he turned and began to swim for the bank brought her to her senses and she ran and began to climb in frantic haste. She felt terrified and unable to analyse why. The sun was hotter than ever, the rocks burning her hands which grew scratched and cut as she hauled herself upwards. Her gown stuck to her and her fair hair was streaked dark. The vision of the spring high in the hills above the treetops was drowned in her terror. Where could she hide from her captor?

She must pause! She wiped the sweat from her face and stared down. To her amazement she saw habitations in the distance. There were villas and gardens where figures toiled, minute from this height. At the edge of the sea was a village and a harbour with boats. Joanna took careful note of the direction. She did not know who owned the villas, but they must be law-abiding folk who would succour her against brutal buccaneers.

She came upon a path leading in the direction of the villas and stepped on it, her heart thumping with anticipation, then gasped as a hand grasped her.

'Not so fast,' said Kester.

She struggled to escape. 'Let me go! Let me go you . . . you devil!'

He held her tighter, both her arms gripped by his hands. The more she fought the more his amusement showed in his saturnine face. 'As a Puritan you probably know more about the devil than most,' he taunted.

She kicked out at him and her shoe caught his bare ankle. He swore. 'I think you need another lesson,' he grated.

Seeing his intention Joanna stopped moving abruptly. 'Sir, I beg of you . . . I will fight you no more . . . please . . . please . . .'

It was as if she had not spoken. Relentlessly his head came down. She twisted from side to side, until with a

swift movement he caught both her wrists in one of his
big hands and used the other to grasp her chin. Then his
mouth was on hers, searching, moving, dragging from
her that terrible ache to respond. When he raised his
head she was still and drained. A pulse pounded in her
forehead and heat consumed her body. She gave a
moan.

His voice was soft. 'How beautiful you are,' he
murmured.

At once her terror increased. She could not fathom
why she found his gentleness more frightening than his
ferocity. She opened her eyes and realised that except
for his breeches he was naked. His hair was still wet, his
feet bare. How tough he must be to have run up the
mountain without shirt or boots.

She remained silent, staring into his face with wide,
agonised blue eyes. For a long moment he continued
to hold her to him, then he released her and she almost
fell.

He threw out an arm towards the villas. 'Were you
thinking of trying to reach them?'

He did not care that she refused to answer. 'It is a good
thing I was able to stop you. You might have happened
on a charitable person, but the chances are greater that
you would have been taken in by some planter hungry
for your sort of beauty. They are not short of females;
the island population is plentiful, but *you* would surely
have proved irresistible. Or maybe a slave trader would
have offered to assist you. How do you relish the idea of
parading your charms in the market place? And I
daresay you know that the people down there are
Spaniards! The enemies of your country!'

Joanna's body was aflame. She ignored his tormenting
words and asked for water.

'Is that why you are here?'

'I saw a spring from the ship. I did not know the place
was inhabited.'

'We are on Hispaniola, madam.'

'Do you not fear that the Spaniards will attack your camp? After all, you are British *and* a disreputable pirate.'

His eyes narrowed. 'Privateer, as I told you. I am about my lawful business for England from whom I hold a commission.'

'You do not scorn to take a commission from a land you refuse to re-enter. I think you like your calling and use it as an excuse for tyranny.'

She almost cursed her wayward tongue. She was amazed when instead of an angry response he touched her forehead with a gentle finger. 'You are very hot and distressed. Come, we will find your precious spring.'

He turned to lead the way and Joanna cried out. His back was a horror of criss-crossed scars and red and purple weals. At some time he had been cruelly and repeatedly flogged. Kester turned at her cry and his face darkened.

'I forgot. Usually I do not inflict the disgusting sight on women.'

His deliberately provoking words and grin for once failed to rouse her. She licked her dry lips. 'Who? Who did that awful thing to you?'

'I do not wish to talk of it. Pray precede me. There is a spring at the top of this incline.'

Joanna moved a step, then stopped. 'Oh, Kester, what manner of people would be so brutal?'

For the first time for many days she forgot her own predicament, lost in the agony of a man so fearfully tortured. Her eyes were soft with gentle compassion and his aggression died.

He said in quiet tones. 'How much of my history did Will tell you?'

'I know that your family was killed.'

Kester nodded. 'I was the only survivor. I wished I had died with the others at the time. With the aid of some

friendly Indians we dug graves and buried my loved
ones. I said no prayers. They died with my family. I was
so lost in grief I had no thought for myself and Will was
little better. We were surprised by the Spaniards who
returned to collect our animals for food. At eighteen
years I was big and muscular so I was not killed, but
many times over the years I was to ache for the mercy of
death. They clubbed Will—I thought they had killed
him—and me they chained to a galley oar. Chained me
by the wrist and ankle with other men for five years. We
were stripped and lived like beasts. For the first weeks
the sun burned me until my skin bubbled. At night and
during storms I shook with cold and fever. If I flagged I
was whipped. Their lashes tore at my flesh. Spaniards!
God, how I hate them!'

He was silent for a moment and Joanna scarcely dared
speak, but she longed to know what had happened.
'How did you get away?' she breathed.

'There was a battle. Pirates rammed the galley. I knew
enough to crouch below those terrible oars and survived
when every man on my bench was crushed. The impact
tore loose my chains and I smeared myself with the
blood of my comrades and feigned dead. As the fight
raged I slipped over the side.'

He stared out across the bright hills. 'The clean water
on my body was a sensation I shall never forget. It made
me realise how many years they had stolen from me. I
climbed aboard the pirate's vessel and grabbed a sword
and naked as I was I fought and killed.'

Joanna shuddered and his lips curled back in a wolfish
grin. 'Aye, I was like a beast that day.'

A beast! She saw that his dreadful past had raised
unbreachable barriers between them.

'When the pirates saw how I fought they welcomed
me. When I amassed enough I went on the account. That
means I set up for myself. I have been seven years taking
my revenge and will not be satisfied until I die.'

He did not wait for a reply, but turned and began to climb. She felt a quick flare of resentment at his autocratic assumption that she would follow. All her life she had been treated with care and consideration. Nothing had prepared her for the eruption into her life of the embittered, scarred man who used her like a possession. Yet as if her feet moved independently to her will she found herself scrambling after him up a path which grew steeper until at last they arrived at a spring which bubbled from the rock. Forgetting everything Joanna sank to her knees and cupped her hands in the water. It was cold and soft and she drank, putting her hands into the water again and again until her mouth and body were refreshed as never before.

Kester touched her shoulder. 'We must return to the shore. My seadogs are like children—if they are not watched they quarrel.'

She turned her blue eyes up to him. He was outlined against the azure sky, his hair glinting with metallic gleams in the fierce sun. She surprised a look on his face which made her catch her breath. Slowly she rose and stood inches from him, her bosom rising and falling in an emotion she could not comprehend. She swayed a little and his arms reached out and went round her. His kiss was as gentle as a breeze. There was nothing of passion or desire. It was like the kiss of a young lover for his maid and Joanna was shaken by a storm of anguish.

Kester said softly, 'Joanna—you are bad for me—you undermine the defences I have fashioned.'

As abruptly as he had kissed her he thrust her from him, before taking his fill of the pure water. Then he walked down the rocky path and she followed him, stumbling a little, feeling resentment resurge as he ignored her.

Once back on shore Kester was fully engaged in controlling the petty squabbles between several men and Joanna seated herself on a rock, watched by Claris whose brown eyes burned with jealous fire.

Joanna scarcely noticed her or the activity. She was wrestling with feelings which were tearing her apart. Kester had thrown a shirt over his shoulders and dragged on his boots before descending the hill and now he was everywhere, directing operations, overseeing everything to the last tiny detail. Joanna supposed he must be a successful privateer. What a misspent life! What a pity he should use his gifts to such base ends.

She realised with shock that she had not taken her eyes from him for several minutes, watching every move he made as he gave expert instructions for repairing his ships.

The butchers were busy slaughtering, smoking, salting and boats were loaded with supplies and rowed out to the fire-damaged ship, now looking almost seaworthy. The shore and water was a mass of movement and suddenly Joanna realised she felt very much a part of it. She caught her breath. How easy it was to sink into evil ways! Surely she did not feel a spark of desire to follow the life of this wicked band.

Kester Venn! His name flashed into her brain and seared her with his image. Dear God, but she must escape before he utterly corrupted her. She paced the shore, the hot sand slipping beneath her shoes. Her gown was torn and stuck to her in the heat. She thought of the crystal clear mountain pool and wished she could bathe. How sweet to immerse one's body. Terrifyingly the memory of Kester's suntanned flesh came to torment her. She had never in her life before seen an unclothed male, but she had found him beautiful.

She ran to Kester where he stood gazing upwards at the *Lady Margaret*. 'Give me a task to perform,' she begged.

His eyes were as cold as if he had never held her tenderly, never caressed her lips with his. 'There is nothing here for a woman such as you.' His voice was more abrasive than ever and she stumbled back to the rock and sank on it.

'He will never succumb to a woman like you, save perhaps for a night's pleasure!'

Claris stood before her, her legs apart in their breeches and boots, an ugly grin on her scarlet lips.

Beyond anger, Joanna begged, 'What can I do? Why will he not set me free? He despises me!'

Claris bent over her and whispered, 'You could never understand him, Puritan. He is mine. Our lives are savage and we are as one in our needs. If you wish to escape I'll help you.'

Joanna's mistrust was written clearly in her face and Claris grinned, 'Who better than I? Who has more wish to get rid of you?'

'That is what I thought,' replied Joanna coldly. 'I do not wish to end my days floating in the sea with my throat cut.'

Claris's grin widened. 'You learn fast, but I swear I won't harm you. If I did *he* would be revenged on me.'

'As he will if he discovers you helped me escape. Does not that frighten you?'

Claris shrugged. 'He might beat me and I would love him more. Even death at his hands would be preferable to life without him.'

'I see. If you care nothing for the consequences how should that make me trust you?'

'I know him so well. If he learns you are safe with your own people he'll dismiss you from his mind. But if I harm you he'll surely find out and might punish me in the only way I could not endure. He might send me from him.'

Her voice reached a sibilance which startled Joanna. Claris stared at her arrogantly. 'You'll never understand *my* kind of love, Miss Puritan. Do you want to get away or not?'

Joanna looked into the eager face of the buccaneer woman. She was far from convinced that she could in any way be trusted, but she was growing hourly more desperate to escape from the privateer captain and all the bewildering longings and emotions with which he imbued her.

She kept her voice as steady as possible: 'I want to be free.'

'Be ready then,' said Claris. 'When I call upon you be prepared to follow and obey me without question.'

The triumphant glance she threw back at Joanna as she strode away did nothing to reassure the distraught captive.

CHAPTER
FOUR

JOANNA was rowed to the repaired ship that night.
Kester bade her goodnight from the shore.

'Until we have the treasure safe aboard I shall remain
near it,' he explained.

'Naturally,' flashed Joanna, 'you would not wish to
leave your precious spoil.'

The words had been dragged from her by an uncon-
trollable disappointment that he remained with Claris.
She pushed it to the back of her mind, but it had mani-
fested itself in words which could only antagonise and
she was not surprised when his brows drew together in
the frown she feared.

'Beware, madam,' he warned quietly, 'you have been
mistress of yourself and your destiny in times past, but
here you are a prisoner. Do not push me too far.'

Joanna opened her lips then closed them as Claris
moved into a circle of lamplight and shook her head
warningly, reminding Joanna that she must not provoke
the Raven to action which might spoil her chance of
escape. She climbed into the rowboat, Will Buckley bent
to the oars, and soon she was conducted to a small cabin
above decks where she undressed and went to bed,
reassured by the fact that Will Buckley sprawled across
her door, nursing a loaded pistol.

She lay in the cabin listening to the soft slap-slap of
waves against the hull, the cries of night creatures from
the island. Light from the moon slanted across the floor
and an abrupt break in the peace by a couple of quarrelsome buccaneers was quickly quelled. She thought of
Kester Venn who had only to direct his black frown at
the half-tamed men to obtain immediately subservience

and was suddenly shaken by the awareness that she had
agreed to put herself in the power of a woman who hated
her; once the Raven was not there to protect her she
would be at the mercy of these terrible people.

She shivered, wondering if she should wait until she
could prevail on him to deliver her to New Providence.
She rejected the idea. Had he intended to take her to
Matthias he would by now have done so. And she admitted that he held a dangerous fascination for her, one
which might lead her to believe she should stay. And
surely he would not keep her at a distance much longer!
At present he was amusing himself, watching her virgin
terror as he toyed with her. As soon as Claris had
perfected a plan she would follow it.

Yet she had not expected Claris to act so fast. The
moon had waned and the sun not risen when she realised
that Claris was shaking her awake.

'Hurry, for God's sake!' Claris's teeth were chattering. 'I've sent Will Buckley on a false errand, but the
Raven will know he's been tricked. Put these on and be
quick!'

Infected by Claris's panic Joanna leaped out of the
bunk and reached for the clothes she was offered. Then
she drew back. 'These are men's garments!'

Claris swore. 'Will you destroy us both? Put them on!
You can't wear female garments. Who knows what scum
we shall meet? Better to appear as a man.'

Joanna dragged on the blue canvas breeches, rough
white cotton shirt and waistcoat, and shoved her feet
into coarse woollen stockings and ill-fitting shoes. She
twisted her hair to the top of her head, securing it with a
scarf and followed Claris out on deck and down a rope
ladder to a rowboat. Two men rowed as fast as they
could, while they cast terrified looks at the island, visible
in the dawn light.

Joanna wondered at the men apparently willing to risk
punishment by Kester Venn. They were some of the

roughest of the buccaneer crew and when they rounded a headland and reached a moored sloop both women were pulled aboard with unnecessary handling. The remainder of the crew were no better and Joanna saw with increasing apprehension that several were those who had been most often reprimanded by the Raven.

Claris said as the sloop slipped out to sea, 'You look as if it would crack your face to smile!'

'This expedition is ill-advised. These men are untrustworthy and if Captain Venn catches us he will extract revenge. I am afraid . . .'

Claris grinned. 'Many women would be happy to receive his punishment. As for me, I care only that he shall be my man.'

'How can you control these men?'

'They'll be biddable, never fear. I've pledged them my share of the treasure, but they'll get nothing until I'm ready. I've buried it on Hispaniola.'

'Won't Kester pursue us?'

Claris laughed. 'Oh, aye, he'll follow. Even if he hated your guts he'd come—he can't endure to be thwarted, but it'll take time. You do as I bid and we'll both get what we want.'

Joanna swallowed hard. What did she want? She was frighteningly unsure. She presumed she would join with her betrothed in his kind of life; yet she had only to close her eyes to find Kester's dark face invading her brain, to hear his sardonic laugh, his harsh voice. Everything about him was calculated to repel a gently reared maid and Joanna shrank from the knowledge that she would never forget him as long as she lived.

Claris said, 'He won't catch us so easily. It'll take time to get the brigantine ready and once you're with your own kind he'll leave you be.'

The small, fast sloop skimmed easily over the warm ocean and Joanna lost count of time. She slept uneasily, guarded by Claris who rested in short catnaps and ignored all questions. The food was rock hard biscuit soaked in rum to soften it and once a day the slovenly cook served a greasy stew. He was impervious to insults about his cooking and Joanna gathered from lewd comments that he was planning to retire to Jamaica where he had a woman and children.

When the sloop reached an island Joanna's heart beat fast. The land rose in a turtle shape and was thickly wooded and she wondered which part was farmed by her future husband.

'Is this our destination?' she asked Claris.

The red-haired girl grinned. 'That's right. Soon you'll learn your fate, eh?'

Joanna spoke her thanks through stiff lips. A sickness seemed to be spreading through her body. Damn Kester Venn! Her heart sank at her profane slip of the tongue. Why must she think of a man who overturned all her teaching?

'How do we get ashore?' she asked abruptly.

'We shall come to a small harbour.'

'Are you not afraid of the authorities? New Providence is law-abiding.'

Claris's laugh could scarcely have been bettered by her master. 'Law-abiding! What know you of the islands? There is only one law out here and that is strength! Is your man strong?'

Joanna thought of her betrothed. At thirty-eight years of age Master Matthias Kemp was almost as much of a scholar as her father. Only direst necessity after the Civil War had forced him abroad to seek a livelihood and she recalled how they had pored over the writing of men anxious to populate the colonies. According to them the Indies were full of lush farms and magnificent plantations.

Matthias's pale face had assumed a little colour as he enthused. 'Think of it, Joanna, tobacco and ginger, sugar and spices, indigo and cocoa, all to be had so easily. There is a fortune to be made.' He had checked himself. 'Of course I do not hold wealth to be important, but a man must live and I look forward to making a home for you.' How had he fared, her man of learning, in this alien world?

Claris was watching her and Joanna was startled to catch a look of spite. Never mind! Claris would soon go and they would never meet again and she would forget Kester Venn.

Claris insisted on going ashore first and Joanna tried to stay calm beneath the stares of the men who reminded her of dogs in a street who had cornered a female. She looked ashore, concentrating on a cluster of huts, praying that soon she would see the girl she was forced to trust, or the form of Master Kemp looking out for her.

A big man who had lost three fingers of his left hand in a fight sidled near, assessing her with bloodshot eyes. 'Josh Harris is the name, mistress. How about casting your lot in with me?'

Joanna strove to sound rational. 'I shall soon be with my affianced husband, Master Harris. You . . . you would not wish to part two whose union has been arranged before God.'

'I'd risk damnation for an armful like you,' he leered, and reached for her.

Joanna slid away and pointed to the shore. 'Claris is returning.'

The man spat and swore, but retreated, and Claris climbed back on board, her eyes darting about, missing nothing of Joanna's flush and Josh Harris's scowl.

'Come on,' she ordered Joanna, 'I've arranged everything.'

Joanna almost sagged with relief. 'I am to go ashore? Master Kemp awaits me?'

Claris merely jerked her head towards the boat and Joanna scrambled down the rope ladder and seated herself and was pulled ashore. She tried to relate the descriptions in Matthias's letters and failed. Perhaps this was a smaller harbour in a different part of New Providence. Of course, Claris would not dare go to a lawful place where she could be apprehended as a pirate.

Joanna stepped ashore and looked about her. She recognised no one and was immediately aware that not one of the persons who watched her was to be trusted.

She followed Claris along a track between a community of roughly-built shacks and shabby tents. The only stone buildings were taverns busy with men and women who reeled in and out with raucous noise. Joanna tried to stride like a man and must have succeeded as no one paid her particular attention. She was accompanied by all but one of the buccaneers and she realised that, scum though they had seemed, the Raven had picked men above those who were the dregs of the Caribbean. There were men here who made Josh Harris look respectable. And the women in their gaudy striped skirts and heavily frilled hats were beyond any female she could have imagined.

The track led through dark jungle before they came upon another shore and Joanna shrank back, causing Harris to prod her into moving again. There were more tents and shacks and the people here were even worse. Several called to Claris who answered in a variety of tongues. Joanna wondered that the law-abiding citizens of New Providence allowed such dissipation.

They halted before a tavern and Claris pushed Joanna. 'Go on in!'

Joanna shook her head. 'I have *never* entered such a place. Master Kemp *cannot* be in there.'

Claris laughed. 'In the Caribbean men are forced into unaccustomed ways.'

'Even if that is true he would not expect me to enter.'

There were shrieks of mirth from within, the door opened emitting a stench of tobacco smoke and stale wine, and a woman erupted, shamefully drunk, dancing, her red and green skirt held high to reveal plump legs encased in blue and green striped stockings with red garters.

Joanna was mesmerised in horror. Never had she visualised such brazen immodesty, but the men only yelled instructions to the whore which Joanna did not understand, but had no difficulty in recognising as vulgar. Claris merely laughed.

When the woman had danced out of sight she nodded at the tavern door. 'Go in,' she commanded.

When Joanna resisted further she was sent staggering by a push from Josh Harris and almost fell through the doorway into a murky interior where she was subjected to a barrage of mirth and she knew finally she had been tricked. She was led into an inner room where she was left with Claris and a man who filled her with unimaginable terror.

He was massively fat, his chin descending in rolls to his white, glutinous chest which was revealed by an open shirt. Sweat rolled down him in the hot, close atmosphere and his face glistened. His hair was thin and pale on a dome-like head, but his eyes, almost black, were petrifyingly alive in his lardy countenance as they flickered over Joanna.

'Take off the scarf,' he ordered, and Claris dragged away the concealing turban, allowing Joanna's hair to tumble down her back, a rippling stream of gold.

'What's her body like?'

Joanna was shaken by a shuddering horror at his tone which was that of a man discussing a beast. Only he was talking of her!

'She's a sweet armful for a man,' grinned Claris. 'Much the same shape as me, but more meat on her.'

The man's tongue ran quickly round his fleshy mouth. 'Good!' he approved. 'You're a bit thin for my taste.'

Joanna turned to Claris. 'For the love of God!' she breathed. 'You do not mean to give me to *him*!'

'Don't you like me, my dear?' A rumbling laugh rolled from the man and his white body shook. 'Well, you needn't fear me. I've had my fill of wenches. I have a better use for them now.'

Joanna clutched at Claris's arm in desperation. 'I beg of you . . . you are an Englishwoman . . . you cannot mean to abandon me to *him*!'

Claris shook off her hands savagely, striking out when Joanna resisted. 'You all but took my man from me. Think you he would truly have let you go? No one takes what belongs to him. I've been his woman nigh on three years and he's not taken another, but I've seen how he looks at you. And you're a maiden, pure and unsullied, not like me who was deceived almost in childhood and abandoned by a scoundrel. The Raven took no heed of my past. I thought he'd marry me, but he'll never do it while you're around him.'

'I will go back to England—I will never trouble you again—only do not leave me here.'

Claris shook her head. 'There's only one sure way to put you out of reach and that's to see he can't pine for your purity any longer. Captain Bowler will see to that.'

Joanna made a further anguished plea. 'Captain Bowler, will you not contact my future husband? He will save me.'

The man's eyes glittered. 'He's rich, this man of yours?'

Joanna spoke eagerly. 'He seems to have prospered. I know he would pay any sum to free me.'

The man stroked his damp chins and regarded her reflectively. 'I wonder how much he can afford. Can he be easily contacted?'

'Indeed, he can, since he is on this island!'

The thin brows rose. 'I had no idea! What is his business?'

'Have done!' Claris sprang between them. 'You know he's not here, but on New Providence!'

'Where are we?' The question came in an agonised wail from Joanna who dreaded the reply.

'This is Tortuga,' cried Claris. 'You'll not see your doughty Puritan gentleman again, so best resign yourself.'

Captain Bowler chuckled evilly and Joanna realised that he had been playing with her, extracting as much amusement from her misery as possible.

'Tortuga!' she breathed. 'Captain Venn once spoke of this place. It is infested, he said, by the sewer rats of the Caribbean. The most degenerate pirates and cut-throats make this their landfall.'

The name of the Raven hovered in the air and for a moment dominated the occupants of the room as his presence would have done. Captain Bowler gave a quick intake of breath; Claris looked nervous and Joanna felt an upsurge of hope. Perhaps even now they would fear his vengeance too much to harm her further.

Hope was quickly destroyed as Claris spat, 'He'll not save you! Even if he tries he'll not get here in time. You're to be sold tonight to the highest bidder and within moments of the sale your precious virginity will be defiled, then you, madam, will be on my level and the Raven can choose, if he wishes, between two women of equally low status. He'll no doubt remember that I've plenty to offer in his kind of life while you've got nothing!'

Captain Bowler suddenly grew bored. He reached down and pulled out a chinking bag from a box near his feet, counted out coins and dropped them into a leather pouch which he handed to Claris. She stuffed it into a large pocket in her baggy breeches.

'An't you going to count them, my dear?' asked the captain.

'I'll take your word there's eighty pieces of eight. You'll make a good profit on her.' Claris stepped back and gave Joanna a malignant stare. 'They'll have seen nothing like her for many a long day—if ever, knowing that scum.'

Joanna tried to speak, to make a last plea for mercy, but her mouth was dry, her lips stiff with horror. Beneath the onslaught of despair and the noxious atmosphere her mind was clouding over.

Claris opened the door to slip away. 'Best get her to the market,' she advised and was gone.

Joanna fought for coherence and made a dart for the door. From the deep shadows in a corner of the room, as dark as the corner from which she rose and almost as fleshy as Captain Bowler, stood a woman who filled Joanna with revulsion, as she stood, hands on enormous hips, grinning at the prisoner.

There was a swift movement, a click, and Joanna found her wrists manacled. The woman opened the door and yelled and two others came and took a rope and twisted it round the manacles and pulled. Joanna followed them, through the tavern where she was subjected to a barrage of insults, outside and along the track, until they came to a clearing. A large cage of spiked wood had been erected and Joanna was thrust inside and the door secured behind her.

There were others there. Several women, manacled as she was, were free to wander, but the men who outnumbered the women were fastened to heavy poles in the ground. She was greeted by several, some of whom appeared to view their fate philosophically, some rebelliously, but not one offered a sign of sympathy or fellow-feeling. Joanna wandered to the far end of the cage, shrinking as far as possible from notice, staring through the bars at the noisy scenes outside. What she saw made her think of the account of hell. The sun was setting redly and fires were alight, giving everything a crimson glow. Drunkenness was clearly accepted here as a normal state and both men and women reeled about, either quarrelling, or displaying passion with a complete lack of reserve. One man presided over an enormous cooking pot into which he was hurling all manner of meats and fowl, inadequately cleaned or plucked, following them with vegetables, pickles and spices and producing an aroma to turn the stomach of anyone not inured to it.

A group was holding a mock trial in obscene imitation of an Admiralty court. One man perched in a mangrove tree, a shaggy hat depicting a wig, while others played the parts of bailiffs and prisoner and, amid much laughter, a man was condemned to be hanged and the punishment feigned in waves of grim laughter in which the 'prisoner' joined. The whole performance was toasted in copious drink.

'They do it out of fear against the day it may happen.'

Joanna whirled at the voice in her ear. A woman in a tattered yellow gown stood by her. 'I'm Jess,' she offered.

'Are you to be sold?' gasped Joanna.

'That's the idea!' Jess shrieked with mirth. 'I stole Cap'n Borgne-Fesse's purse while he slept. This is my punishment.'

'Does no one care for *anyone* here?'

Jess shrugged. 'He could have had me flogged and didn't. Like as not he'll get his temper back and buy me. If not, well, one man's same as another between the sheets.'

Joanna was shaken by a wave of terror and Jess peered at her. 'You're not the usual kind they get here. What you done?'

'I—upset a woman,' said Joanna flatly.

Jess nodded. 'I see. She must be a really nasty cow to do this to you. Still, with your looks you'll soon go and maybe your master will treat you fair. You'll have to learn to cosset him.'

'These men do not know the meaning of the word fair. They are without honour.'

'I wouldn't say that.' Jess pointed through the bars.

'See them? They're swearing the rules of piracy over an axe. They got rules, d'you see, and they most often abide by them.'

Their conversation was cut short by the two women guards who had brought Joanna to the cage. One unshackled her wrists and the other held out a garment. 'Take off those men's things and put this on and be quick. Sale's about to begin.'

Joanna looked at the tawdry gown of orange and scarlet striped satin adorned by many blue bows and turned aside, clutching her seaman's shirt. The rougher of the women grabbed her arms viciously tight. 'Change your raiment or we'll do it for you.'

Sudden silence fell in the compound and Joanna saw the eyes of the shackled men gleaming expectantly. She said quaveringly, 'Please—is there somewhere private I can change?'

'Let's make a shield for her,' volunteered Jess.

'What for?' snarled the guard. 'She'd best get used to showing herself off!'

But the other woman co-operated with Jess and Joanna crouched behind the two women, dragging off breeches and shirt and pulling the gown over her head. Jess fastened the tapes and buttons and Joanna stood before them in a gown which moulded her figure, emphasising every curve, and was shamefully revealing.

'Take off your shoes and stockings,' ordered the guard, 'they don't go with the dress.'

Past speech Joanna obeyed and found she was to be led to the slave market in bare feet. The manacles were snapped back on and she leaned against the bars, awaiting the inevitable outcome in helpless despair.

The men in prime condition were sold first. She watched them prodded and kicked to a space in a large circle of men and recognised the voice of the auctioneer. Captain Bowler played many parts, it seemed.

Jess was removed, grinning and winking, and Joanna

shrank from the roars of merriment as she was sold. Then it was her turn.

All the gloating faces were a blur as she stumbled to the clearing. She was forced up on to a wooden platform before the raised chair of the auctioneer who began to laud her charms.

The first appreciative waves of laughter died away as the men contemplated Joanna's perfect young figure and pure ashen face. There was a rustle of movement in the crowd which parted to allow the progress to the front of several men of higher stature.

Captain Bowler greeted them, his gloating anticipation of a good sale larding his voice, 'Ah, my good captains, I thought this one would interest you. Captain Borgne-Fesse, you've just lost your woman and will be needing someone to warm your bed. Who better than this luscious piece?'

A burst of encouraging laughter came from the surrounding men and he continued, 'And she's a maiden, my captains, as pure as the day she left her mother.'

Several rejoinders of lewd wit left him imperturbable. 'Oh, aye, she's a maid. A Puritan girl taken by one of your brothers and now to be sold.'

'Any man who'd rid himself of such a prize is mad—or she's got hidden pitfalls.'

'That's true,' agreed a black-bearded man with a scarred face. 'Are you trying to get rid of a poxy wench?'

Captain Bowler spread his hands. 'Gentlemen! You have my word on't, though it shouldn't be necessary. Haven't you found me trustworthy?'

The black-bearded one growled that if he for one purchased a woman and found the goods to be damaged he would bring them back and Bowler would know the weight of his anger, but the other men proclaimed the captain to be an honest tradesman.

Joanna's lacerated feelings at hearing herself described as so much merchandise were ravaged still further when the men strolled nearer and walked around her. Then one shoved a rough forefinger beneath her chin and forced up her head. She stared in terror into the face which leered into hers and her degradation and horror were complete when she recognised Captain Pryce.

'This woman's mine!' he yelled, looking at the other men in an effort to extract sympathy, 'filched from me by that dog Captain Venn!'

The Raven! The words rippled through the company and two of the captains stepped away smartly. 'If she's the Raven's woman I want no part in stealing her.'

Captain Bowler was soothing. 'Now, gentlemen, would she be on my auction block illegally? You know I abide by your rules. She was brought to me by his own lieutenant. It seems he wants no part of a Puritan wench. We all know his story. He believes his revenge will be the better for having her sold.'

Captain Borgne-Fesse said in his heavily accented voice, 'Why would he sell her unless he's had his fill of her? How can she be a maiden?'

'To hell with all that!' Captain Pryce's bellow cut through the discussion. 'I offer a hundred pieces of eight for the wench, virgin or not, for the pleasure of her body.'

Argument forgotten, the bidding became brisk, even the two reluctant men seeing such a prize sliding from them, joining in.

Two hundred pieces of eight, five hundred, the bids grew higher as rivalry increased and the silence over the compound became profound. It seemed as if everyone in that hellish company was mesmerised by the incredible sale.

The bidding stopped at six hundred and fifty pieces of eight and Captain Bowler failed to raise it. One of his women stepped forward at a nod and lifted Joanna's gleaming rope of hair and allowed it to fall so that it floated and shimmered over her shoulders like a gold cloak in the light from the flaring candlewood branches.

The other woman dragged back the skirts of her gown until it was skin tight, revealing her lovely outline.

The bidding began again, though more slowly, until Captain Pryce said loudly, 'Seven hundred I bid! It's a damnable price considering she was mine by virtue of spoil, but I mean to have her.'

Joanna's senses swam. She believed that almost anyone would be better than he. She had pinned her hopes, if she must be sold, to one of the more moderate sounding men.

But no one raised the bid and Captain Bowler's hammer was poised when a cool voice cut across the compound. 'Eight hundred pieces of eight!'

There was a gasp, a murmur, heads turned to the shadows beyond the circle and Joanna lifted her head in disbelief.

Claris had said that he could never arrive in time to save her, but by some incredible feat of seamanship he was here. He stepped between the men who made way for him hastily. When he reached the centre he bowed courteously, 'Good evening, gentlemen. I apologise for my tardy arrival. I was delayed.'

He received answering bows, even from Pryce, whose eyes glittered evilly. 'Why bid for the wench after sending her to market?' he enquired with a leer.

The Raven's eyes flickered coldly over Joanna. 'A man is permitted to change his mind.'

Captain Bowler's tongue licked his fleshy lips. 'Your lieutenant had permission to dispose of the woman, didn't she, sir?'

The Raven's lip curled at the unctuous tone. 'How— thoughtful of you to enquire.'

He made no attempt to answer the question. Even in these hideous circumstances he remained publicly loyal to his shipmate. He waited, his eyes turned expectantly to the auctioneer. 'Proceed with your business, sir.'

Captain Bowler was hoarse. 'Any more bids, gentlemen?'

Captain Pryce said, almost in a whisper, 'Nine . . . nine hundred.'

The Raven's voice was without inflexion. 'One thousand.'

'Damn you to hell!' Captain Pryce looked his hatred. 'How ever high I go you intend to raise me.'

'One day,' articulated the Raven, 'you and I must have an account. There is the matter of a ship.'

'I took this woman in fair fight,' blustered Pryce.

'You took her during an attack on a defenceless British merchantman, and abandoned her in your haste to escape my retribution for the stealing of my vessel.'

Joanna burned with shame. Was she simply a pawn in their devious game of cut and thrust?

Captain Pryce turned and stumped through the watching pirates, kicking any who got in his way.

The hammer descended and the rope was handed to Captain Venn who immediately passed it to Will Buckley.

'Take her to my ship,' commanded the Raven, and walked off, calling to several other captains who joined him with loud laughs, and Joanna was led away like a beast from a market.

CHAPTER
FIVE

SHE was unable to raise her eyes as she was led between the ranks of men who silently acknowledged her to be the property of the man who had publicly purchased her.

Will struck out along a path beneath closely hanging trees. Joanna ducked helplessly, unable to brush the vines aside with her imprisoned hands. Her feet were tormented by unseen obstacles on the jungle path and she gasped as she stepped on a cruelly sharp thorn.

'Please, Will,' she begged, 'have you lost all your kindness? My feet are bare—my face will be cut . . .'

At this he halted, lifting his lamp, and she saw his face set in angry, reproachful lines, his eyes cool. 'My master would not want you damaged.'

He put his fingers to his mouth and emitted a low whistle. Other men appeared, one of whom gave Joanna his shoes. Will released one of her hands. She wondered why the men had apparently stayed concealed in the trees and asked Will, but he ignored her. She stalked after him, the ill-fitting shoes rubbing her heels and ankles. Seething with impotent fury, her first gratitude at her rescue was supplanted now by humiliation and rage. She supposed the Raven had sent her off with his buccaneers so that he might enjoy the doubtful pleasures offered by Tortuga. Her lip curled, before she acknowledged that the disgust she felt towards the Raven was as nothing to her self-contempt when she admitted that she loathed the idea of another woman in his arms.

They rowed out to the ship which was moored off a rocky cove. She climbed aboard and the crew crowded around Will, asking questions, grumbling at their master's refusal to allow them on the island for a night.

But Kester had picked his men well, and apart from allowing their eyes to explore Joanna's exposed charms in a way which shamed her, they left her alone.

Will conducted her to the cabin and turned to leave, but she caught his arm. 'Why will you not speak to me? I thought we were friends.'

'You can ask me that, mistress? My master's done you no wrong yet you run off and put him to all the trouble of chasing you. He's had to change his plans.'

Joanna stepped back, her face flaming. 'Has he, indeed! And what of me? I had a plan to wed my betrothed, and your master cares nothing for my wrecked life!'

'It ain't his fault you was taken off the merchantman, and he stopped you from being hurt by Pryce, yes, and saved you again today.'

'I was—I am grateful for his help, but now he should restore me to my own world.'

Will shrugged. 'You're lucky he bothered to come after you this time when you treat him badly.'

He stepped through the door and locked it behind him. Joanna took off the hateful gown and slid, naked, into the bunk, too exhausted to think further. She slept heavily, stirring only when she caught the sound of movement from the outer cabin. She heard Kester's murmurs and Will's, and lay rigid, expecting the Raven to burst in, but the voices went quiet and she knew that Kester slept.

In the morning Will brought clothes. 'Master says to join him for breakfast.'

They had sailed during the night and the window revealed the blue sea beneath a cloudless sky. The air was soft, but no softer than the silk of the fresh clothes. There was a tobacco-brown overdress which looped back over a blue-green petticoat. She drew on silk stockings tied with red ribbon garters. Her hands shook. Had *he* chosen them; or had Will been deputed to bring her the sensuous pleasure of silk. She shook her head, trying to dislodge her unmaidenly thoughts, ashamed when she recalled her parents' warnings about royalist unseemliness.

Anger with herself made her take a dislike to the many knots of ribbons adorning the gown and she bit through the thread savagely and threw them away. Then she slid her feet into a pair of long, pointed kid shoes and was tugging recklessly at the brown silk roses decorating them when a sound made her raise her head.

The Raven was leaning by the door, watching her. He looked at the heap of ribbons then at Joanna who straightened, trying to meet his eyes which flickered over her in cool disdain.

'A gentleman would knock before entering a lady's chamber,' she rasped, her voice all the more contemptuous because of the wanton stirring of that strange longing with which he imbued her.

She was answered by a harsh laugh. 'You give yourself airs and graces, madam, considering you are mine more than ever now.'

'How so?'

'Once you were my possession by capture—now you are my slave by purchase.'

Joanna gasped. 'Oh, God, you surely do not mean to use such barbaric reasoning!'

'Do I not?' His dark eyes raked her and a sardonic smile touched his lips briefly. 'Why not?'

'Because you are still a man of birth and breeding in spite of . . .' She stopped, alarmed by the dangerous gleam in his eyes.

'Pray, continue. In spite of—what?'

'Of your—fall from grace.'

'Grace!' The laugh rang through the cabin. 'All grace finished for me many years ago in a lonely cove.'

Joanna stared into the dark face, wondering if she could touch his heart. 'Kester, many have suffered—

some more than you—they do not spend a lifetime seeking revenge.'

His blazing fury sent shivers over her. 'You dare to preach to me! You *are* a canting Puritan, after all. I wondered lately, at times, if your church's teaching had fallen on somewhat stony ground.' He stepped close and she found it difficult not to shrink back as his male dominance overwhelmed her. 'What know you of suffering?'

'Little enough,' she blazed, 'but is that my fault? It appears that you intend to teach me enough for my lifetime.'

For a moment blue eyes and brown were locked in angry duel, then she looked away, defeated. She took a step towards the door and instantly he grasped her arm. She stopped, sensing an emotion she could not analyse, unwilling to provoke him further.

His eyes were on the discarded ribbons. 'You have spurned my choice!'

So he had chosen the garments himself! 'Not so, sir,' she replied in low tones. 'I am wearing the dress.'

'But without the adornments. Do you set yourself up to be above the women of my world?'

Deliberately misunderstanding him, she forgot caution. 'I do, sir. I am far above the creatures with whom I have been forced into contact.'

He dropped her arm and his hand brushed his brow. 'I did not mean to insult you, Joanna. I was thinking of other women of days gone by. They did not scorn . . . Damn the ribbons! Leave them if you wish.'

Instantly Joanna wished she had been more gracious, especially when Kester drew a length of diaphanous blue-green silk from his pocket. 'A kerchief for your bodice.'

Joanna's hand went to her neck and she became aware with a shock that she had remained unheeding of the brevity of her bodice. Was it so easy to slide into depraved ways? Yet she owed him something for her rejection of the ribbons. 'A royalist lady would not mind the low cut of the gown. I . . . . I will not alter it.'

He continued to hold out the swathe of silk. 'You will wear it!'

She lifted her deep blue eyes to his and slowly a flush spread over her face. 'I see. Now I am in truth your property you do not wish me to be ogled by your men.'

An irrational disappointment brought pricking tears to her eyes. She would not weep before him, but the effort of fighting the tears held her still and his face grew dark with anger. Abruptly he took the silk and twisted it about her shoulders. With ungentle hands he tucked the ends into the front of her bodice and had finished almost before she was aware of his touch scorching her breast.

'Now, madam, you will walk with me on deck and you will look happy to be with me or, by God, I'll beat you!'

The flush died, leaving her white. 'Very well, *master*, I will obey,' she flashed, her voice glacial.

She strode swiftly past him and he followed her on deck and together they paced the ship, talking of trivialities as if they trod a village street. The buccaneers watched them intently. She supposed that they would not be surprised either by her flight or by her apparent obedience now. Their own lives were equally immoderate and irrational. If the Raven beat her she knew they would accept that also. What wild, dangerous men they were. Suddenly she thought of Matthias on New Providence. How had he fared? Had he been forced to compromise by evil? He had not mentioned such matters in his rare letters. She glanced sideways at her captor. His black hair blew in the soft, cooling breeze. His profile, etched against a lazy white sail, was dark and chiselled. *He* would never compromise. She was ashamed of the way she had immediately compared him with Matthias, to the latter's detriment.

They stopped on the forecastle and looked out over

the waves. A huge shoal of fish darted just below the surface with ten thousand silver gleams, and vanished. The wind carried scents of unfamiliar blooms from one of the many tiny cays which could make sailing these waters so hazardous to some; such a haven for pirates who knew them well and could find refuge or an attacking base in the countless coves and inlets.

She sighed and said in a gentle voice, 'Kester, I make another plea. My family will be distraught when they hear I am missing and Matthias—he needs me.'

'*He* needs you! What of me?'

She gave him a quick, startled look. His dark eyes held an expression which made her heart race. Was this another amusing game? Was he trying to soften her towards his conquest?

She was persuasive. 'You do not need me. You are strong, rich and clever . . .'

He gave her a small bow of acknowledgement and she continued, 'Matthias is not robust or possessed of great wit. But he is a good man and has striven to prepare my home. He . . . he loves me . . . in his way, and I . . . I care for him.'

'Care for him! Loves me in his way!' The Raven's voice was as mocking as ever. 'Is that what you desire? By heaven, I do not believe it. You were fashioned for a real man. Will you hide that loveliness in a Puritan society which will make you cover it? The women because they envy it and the men lest they slaver after your flesh in a way denied by their own prudishness.'

Joanna said angrily, 'You are unfair! It is not at all like that! They are good folk and they are mine. I want nothing of your evil life.'

She tried to leave the forecastle and he put out a restraining hand. 'Smile, Joanna, we are being watched.'

So, with her lips stretched over a false grimace, she

returned to the cabin where she sat in her silken gown, waiting to see what her owner had in store for her. The hours dragged by. There was nothing on this ship to read, nothing for her to do. She could only think and she found it unbearable. She tried to escape by going out on deck where men stopped work to stare at her and there were whistles and shouts.

The Raven came silently behind her and spoke in an undertone. 'How dare you leave the cabin without permission. Return to it.'

She took a tentative step forward, then froze as he said, 'Obey me, madam, or it will be the worse for you.'

At this she turned, but her angry protest died when she met his eyes, cold with rage. Fear and misery mingled and she put out a supplicating hand. 'Please—I am going mad shut up with no occupation.'

'Go back!' he ordered, and with a sob she sped back to the confines of the cabin.

She had not realised he had followed her until he said close to her ear, 'If you disobey me again in this matter I shall have you put below decks where you will learn what true imprisonment means.'

'Kester,' she begged, 'why are you being so implacable?'

'You can ask that, after you crept away in the night with Claris, away from my protection? Have I not treated you humanely?'

She made a pleading movement with her hands. 'You have not harmed me, but you hold me captive. You will not set me free to go about my lawful pursuits. You cannot blame me for seeking to return to my proper existence.'

'Blame you!' He stepped close and she found it difficult not to shrink from his suddenly blazing fury. 'If I had not come upon you when I did where would you be now? I will tell you. You would be in Pryce's bed! He has the reputation of a street cat—you would not have been discarded until your pride was destroyed, your hope utterly confounded, your body desecrated. And then he would have sold you again—or handed you to a couple of favoured seamen.'

She gave a moan and he laughed harshly. 'You should be on your knees thanking me, yet still you follow your wilful way and tempt my buccaneers.'

At this her head went up. 'I do not want to be here. I owe you gratitude, it is true, for taking me from him, but you should complete your task and restore me to my loved ones.'

'Ah, yes, Matthias, who loves you in his way. Are you aflame to join him, this lover of yours?'

'All right,' she flared, 'mock him. He will never perhaps be strong like you, but he is a man of quiet integrity. You have chosen to renounce your upbringing and the paths of decency; must you sully all who come into contact with you?'

'Have I sullied you, Joanna?' His voice was as gentle as a whisper, his dark eyes were half closed, containing a teasing warmth.

She felt the familiar weakness stealing over her, and was torn by her own frailty. There was a constricting lump in her throat and she could only stare at him from wide, shadowed blue eyes.

He touched her soft cheek with one finger, stroking her to her chin, continuing to her neck and down to the soft whiteness where the gauze scarf concealed her beauty. It took all her resolution not to sway to him and she was horrified by the unbidden words in her brain, words of pleading that he would hold her close.

Invaded by the terror of her desire, she stepped back, knocking his hand away. Her words were half-choked. 'You sully me now, in your unsought touch. No man has ever ventured to lay his hand on me, save you.'

He showed white teeth in a caustic grin. 'Least of all

Master Kemp, I dare swear. I cannot reconcile your description of him with the desires of a warm-blooded male.'

Joanna bit her lip. Whatever she said only provoked him to further barbs at the expense of herself and her betrothed.

'Have you no more words for me, mistress? Very well. I will return to my duties.'

He was gone and Joanna sank to a bench, her knees refusing to support her. How he was enjoying himself, toying with her as a cat toys with a mouse. When would he end her torment, and how? Either by releasing her, or . . . or by what? Making her his next mistress? She was shaken by such conflicting emotions.

For the remainder of the voyage back to Hispaniola the Raven treated her with disdainful courtesy and she was careful not to provoke him. Will Buckley was the only other man allowed to come near her and he thawed towards her, after making one more reproach for her treatment of his beloved master.

She looked pleadingly at him. 'Will, I respect you for your loyalty, but *I* have no kinship with him. Why does he not let me go?'

Will smiled, his face creasing into wrinkles induced by sun and wind. 'Now, don't you be so impatient, Mistress Seldon. He's been turned from a gentle English boy into a rough seadog by those who tried to destroy him, but you remind me of his mother and sisters and I reckon you do the same for him. He's not harmed you, has he, and if he keeps you by him you could have a good life.' He touched his nose with a knowing finger. 'I've got my hopes, mistress.'

They sailed on, rounding the jutting peninsular to the west of Hispaniola, along the south coast of the island. Joanna spent her time staring through the cabin windows at the lush coastline where vegetation proliferated, descending like green waterfalls to the white beaches and often to the sea itself; at the mountains rising into the clear sky.

She took daily walks with the Raven and revelled in the soft, scented breezes, the translucent water which shimmered round the hull, before sweeping inland to break in creamy foam on the shore. Her heart sang for all the beauty. If only there was someone with whom she could share her delight, but Kester held her distant and Will only grinned, still locked in some impossible dream of his own.

They anchored off Hispaniola at noon and Kester swept the beach with his eyeglass. Joanna stood beside him, the breeze whipping her skirts about her legs.

'What do you see?'

He handed her the glass and she closed one eye and peered through. Small, round sections of the land became visible to her. The brigantine was still careened and being worked on. The butchers had completed their preparation for stores and many men lounged and slept. She handed the glass back silently.

'We go ashore,' pronounced the Raven, and moments later Joanna was in a rowboat, watching the island grow closer, her nose drinking in the heady scents which were wafted strongly to her in the midday heat.

Again she stepped on the soft, sandy beach of Hispaniola and was surprised by a swift surge of relief and gratitude that she had been safely brought back. It was followed by chagrin. Where were her proper sentiments? She had been purchased from one rogue by another and should be mourning that she was not safe with Matthias, instead of with the bloodthirsty Brethren of the Coast. She pulled her hat brim down to shield her face, but knew that all the men were staring at her, no doubt surmising whether or not she had received punishment.

Kester seemed to forget her presence as he strode to his ship, her hull showing holes where new planking, fashioned by the carpenters, was being inserted in place of the rotten.

He bent his dark head to listen intently to his craftsmen, nodded in apparent satisfaction, then walked to a hut erected near palms which leaned over the beach. A man guarding the door grinned and flung it open and Kester stepped into the dim interior and closed the door behind him.

For an instant there was silence followed by voices. She was startled and went to Will. 'Is Claris in there? Has she not made good her escape?'

Will gave a grim smile. 'She wasn't to know that the Raven followed you to Tortuga and brought you back. She and the other traitors left the sloop down the coast where they'd stolen it and slipped overland. They were caught by the guards looking out for them.'

Joanna asked, 'How did Captain Venn know where I was?'

Will glanced sideways at her. 'You haven't asked him?'

Joanna turned from his searching stare. 'He . . . he has not been . . . approachable since he . . . saved me.'

Will grunted. 'I've never seen him act the way he did when he found you'd run off with Claris. He was possessed of a demon, but he forced himself to calm down and think. Claris has been saying that you ought to be returned to your affianced husband, hoping, it seems, that the Raven would be led off the right scent. But he knows how jealous she is and he recalled right at the start that she'd said in open council that you ought to be taken to the market at Tortuga and sold and the proceeds divided.'

'What did he say to that?' asked Joanna quietly.

Will laughed. 'He muttered something about a ransom, though to tell truth, mistress, no one believed in the ransom. All the men think that you and he . . .' He stopped, colour reddening his cheeks.

'Well, mistress,' he continued, 'the Raven spoke to me as we sailed for Tortuga in that slow vessel we repaired. He said if Claris had taken you to New Providence you'd be safe, but if she'd gone to that swine, Bowler . . .' He didn't need to say more.

There was a cry of despair from the hut and Joanna's eyes widened. 'What will he do to her?'

Will shrugged. 'Can't say. No one's ever tried to cheat the captain like that before. She certainly hates you.'

Joanna shivered. In this life of lawlessness she never knew when she would be confronted by the uncontrolled passions of people the like of whom she could not have dreamed so short a time ago.

Claris's voice was raised in further distress and Joanna felt sick. Surely Kester was not so far gone in cruelty as to beat a woman. He flung open the door and strode out. Claris dragged at his arms, all pride gone, her face tearful and desperate, her words incoherent. The Raven pulled her hands from him and repulsed her with such force that she reeled back into the hut and the guard, grinning evilly, slammed the door which she began to pound.

Will said, 'He'll never be able to turn her loose in that state. I believe she'd kill you both.'

The men continued work on the brigantine, not stopping through the darkness which they relieved by the light from burning branches of the candlewood tree. Joanna was returned to the ship in the bay at night and allowed to spend her days on the island. She walked about, attended by Will, and grew fascinated by the lush, green beauty, picking her way through tangled vegetation under the great canopy of trees, plucking brilliant crimson and yellow blossoms which flourished in patches of sunlight on the forest edge, watching birds in dazzling plumage, some so tiny she mistook them at first for humming bees.

As the days drifted by she was lulled into a sense of

euphoria and felt a shock when the Raven informed her that they would soon be sailing.

The worries she had pushed aside returned to plague her. 'Where are we going?' she asked brusquely.

He ignored her question and walked away and she stared resentfully at his retreating back. Since her return he had treated her with increasing coldness. Did he blame her for his ruined relationship with his mistress? Anger blazed through her, bewildering and shattering, as she wondered suddenly if he actually spent his nights in the small hut beneath the palm trees.

Joanna's first opinion of her captor had been undergoing an insidious change as she watched how he lived, his meals sparse, his person scrupulously clean, his garments spartan and spotless, his commands and expectations severe, but just. She was lulled into believing him little different from his gently-bred English ancestors until the day before they sailed.

The *Lady Margaret* had been refloated, graceful and serene in the translucent waters of the bay, her swaying masts tall against the sky which merged in the distance into the azure haze of the sea, and Joanna was surprised by a surge of gladness that she would soon step on her white decks again.

Then she saw a boat rowed from the smaller vessel and the men who had helped Claris abduct her were led ashore, their hands and feet in irons. They clanked over the sand to a circle of men who parted to allow them through. There were mutters of anger against them and no face expressed a particle of pity.

They stopped before the Raven who sat on a dais of logs.

'What will happen to them?' whispered Joanna to Will.

He hushed her to silence as the Raven spoke. He talked of the rules of brotherhood the men had sworn over an axe, of their treachery, their dishonesty in purloining a spoil of the sea from which in time all should benefit.

In her new-found optimism it took Joanna a few moments to comprehend exactly what he meant and her face burned. 'He means me!' she hissed.

Will put out a restraining hand, but she continued, 'He speaks of me! I am the . . . spoil from which they would all have benefited!'

'A manner of speaking, mistress,' muttered Will. 'For God's sake, hush your noise. This court is as sacred as any other.'

Joanna started forward, indignation making her reckless, and Will amazed her by grabbing her from behind and putting a surprisingly strong hand over her mouth. He said desperately in her ear. 'Do you want me to drag you into the jungle? The men are always ripe for sensation. Give them half a chance and they'll see you as a desirable woman. Only respect for the Raven holds them in check.'

Several of those nearest had turned to investigate the scuffle. One frowned and nudged his neighbour and Joanna slumped and Will released her.

The 'court' was conducted with surprising formality, witnesses called and evidence compared. The Raven pronounced judgment. 'You have been found guilty on two counts. You attempted to leave the company knowing full well that our articles say that none shall go out on his own account until each man is possessed of one thousand pounds. And you intended to defraud your companions.' He looked round at the ring of faces. 'The judgment is spoken, gentlemen. What is to be the punishment?'

'Is he going to let those brutes decide?' asked Joanna, her face scornful.

'He's got no choice, mistress,' replied Will. 'He was elected to position of captain, but he holds it only by his strength, wit, and courage in battle, and if he tried to break the rules they'd rise and kill him. All his bravery and cleverness would avail him nothing against this horde.'

Joanna was silenced as one or two shouted suggestions made her blood run cold, but they were ignored by the majority who presumably had some small feeling left towards their former comrades. The men heard their fate with grim, white faces as they were ordered to have ears and noses slit. Joanna fled into the shelter of the forest to escape the gruesome spectacle and Will followed her.

As she leaned against the wide bole of a cedar tree fighting nausea she was joined by Kester and Will slipped away.

'You were watching, Joanna?'

'I was, sir.' Revulsion sharpened her tone to contempt, but he did not rise to it.

'I abhor torture,' he averred quietly. 'I have suffered too much from cruelty myself. In this matter I had no choice.'

'So Will explained. It makes it all the more reprehensible that you remain with these vile creatures.'

He was silent and she stole a glance at his face which contained a measure of sadness. Her fury waned. 'Kester, cannot you leave them? Accompany me to New Providence—there must be honest work for a man with brains.'

At her soft pleading he touched her hand, allowing his fingers to travel to her wrist. The atmosphere of friendly discourse was rent apart as his hand tightened round her arm and she swayed towards him. For a long moment they stared into one another's eyes, then their rapport was destroyed as shouts and yells rang through the echoing forest.

'The punishment is done,' he muttered, 'I am needed again.'

He marched back, pulling Joanna after him, and to

her horror, the fearful court was convened once more and Claris led before the circle of men, her face arrogant, her lips curved in a defiant grin.

She was in her man's attire of breeches and waistcoat and she stood straight, her head thrown back. 'So, my comrades, deal with me as you will,' she yelled.

Her defiance induced a roar from the men. They admired valour and after a brief hearing it was announced that she would suffer no mutilation, but should be marooned with the others.

Will looked grim as he explained to Joanna that marooning was the most feared of punishments. Men were put ashore on one of the hundreds of tiny, often barren, islands in the Caribbean and left to rot. Before Joanna had time to express disgust that the Raven should allow such an end to a woman he had loved they learned that he had bought mercy with his rights in the prisoners' forfeited booty to which he had added a further large amount.

They were to be left on Hispaniola where they would be in danger from the Spaniards or any hostile buccaneers or Indians who discovered them, but at least they would have a chance of life.

Claris was led away and as she passed Joanna she threw her a look of loathing. 'It's all your fault,' she mouthed. 'I'll not forget you, Madam Puritan. I'll be revenged on you some day.'

Then the pirate who led her jerked on the rope and Claris was taken into the forest. She and the others were abandoned on a lonely shore to await their fate and Joanna and Kester sailed on the brigantine in the early dawn.

CHAPTER
SIX

OUT in the deep waters of the Caribbean Joanna realised with amazement that she felt at home. She tried to suppress such an alien notion. Her place was with her own kind, by the side of her promised man, attending to household duties, following God's commands, worshipping at the Meeting House, raising Matthias's children. The idea was thrust abruptly away. It brought forth other pictures; of herself and Matthias spending all their days together—and nights.

As the mountains of Hispaniola faded from view Kester allowed her to tread the decks as long as she made certain that he or Will was within sight and call. She had glanced quickly at him when he gave her this mark of leniency, appreciating it all the more after her attempt at escape, but his face contained no softness, his eyes no kindness.

Anger had shaken her and she asked, 'Are you not concerned that I may try to escape again?'

She regretted the words instantly. He gave her a long cold stare, then waved his arm out over the ocean. 'You have plans for swimming, madam? Or maybe you think to entice one of my seadogs! How will you do it? With a promise of wealth—or with your sweet, virgin body?'

She recoiled inwardly at his abrasive tone. He seemed to dislike her more than ever. Perhaps her part in removing his mistress from his side was bitterly resented.

She gasped, 'If you hate me so much why do you not take me to New Providence and be rid of of me?'

His brows drew together. 'I will tell you when I have decided your future,' he rasped, and strode away, snapping orders to his men.

Joanna seated herself on a pile of rope and watched him covertly as he conferred with the bo'sun. He wore his usual black and white, but Joanna knew that the cut and style were far removed from the drab garments of her own menfolk. The white lace at his wrists and throat accentuated the brown strength of his face and hands. His muscular shoulders seemed scarcely contained by the dark cloth and Joanna suddenly recalled his body as she had seen it stripped and floating lazily in the mountain pool. She swallowed hard and remembered also the cruel scars on his back. Who was she to judge him harshly?

She wanted to go to him and tell him she was sorry, but the impulse died as quickly as it was born. Sorry for what? And did his own past misfortunes condone his treatment of her now?

Will came to sit by her, puffing at a pipe. She coughed a little at the smoke. 'I never saw anyone use tobacco before,' she smiled, 'though of course I have heard of it.'

Will grinned. 'It's a great comfort to a man and one of the few things I like about the Indians.'

Joanna asked hesitantly, 'How did you join up again with your master? He has told me how he was taken by Spaniards and chained to an oar. What became of you?'

Will blew a cloud of smoke and stared out to sea. Then he said, 'I was hit on the head. I wasn't completely unconscious, though I couldn't move. I knew they'd taken my young master alive. They fired the house again and left me for dead. I had to lie for a long time listening to the crackle of flames, wondering if I was doomed to die a lingering death, then rain came. Thank God, it was a heavy downpour and perhaps it helped revive me. I don't know, but I found the use of my limbs returning. I was able to crawl and put out the last of the flames. I managed to save what was left of the house. It wasn't much, but the kitchen was still sheltered. Even the fire still burned in the range. That was funny, wasn't it, mistress? I don't know how long I lay before the fire. I could reach a jug of milk on the table and that sustained me. By slow degrees I got my strength back.'

'How dreadful,' breathed Joanna. 'And there was a Bible . . . Captain Venn allows me to read it.'

'Aye! The only book saved from the fire. It was in the master's tin box with the family papers. Singed, but still readable.'

Again there was a pause and Will said, 'By the time I could move about properly it was well into winter and I made secure what I could and lived on a few stores. Then I decided to stay where I was. I always hoped the young master would come back and anyways, I didn't have anywhere else to go. I cultivated a bit of ground and sure enough Master Kester returned. He was changed from the gentle, loving boy I remembered, but I owed him a duty then as now. He's a good man, Mistress Seldon, though you might find that hard to believe. He's merciful, and that's a rare quality among the Brethren of the Coast.'

They were interrupted by a cry from the lookout man: 'Sail ho!'

Many vessels had been sighted and Joanna had heard the men murmuring against the Raven who refused to stop and indulge in acts of petty piracy, simply for the sake of violence or minor gain. Fortunately the majority of his men agreed with him so they continued on their peaceful way.

'Where are we bound?' asked Joanna.

Will gave her a speculative glance. 'If the master an't told you I don't think I should.'

Joanna shook her head. She had discarded her hat except in the noonday heat and her hair gleamed in the sun with a thousand lights. Her complexion was assuming a golden tan which enhanced the blue of her eyes. She realised that the Raven had stopped talking to look at her and for a moment she caught a flicker of something in his face which made her heart pound. He sauntered towards her, his expression grim, the lines etched between nose and chin pronounced.

He jerked his head at Will who scurried away.

Joanna protested, 'You treat him like a dog! He has been loyal to you and yours.'

Kester seated himself beside her, stretching out his long legs in their black leather boots, as shiny and immaculate as if he had been going to court. The sight infuriated Joanna still further. 'I suppose you obtain your pretty garments from your robberies,' she said.

The dark brows rose. 'I see you are in one of your quarrelsome moods. Would you prefer me to garb myself like my men?'

Joanna glanced about her at the dozens of men who inhabited the ship. They wore an astonishing array of garments in every imaginable colour. Many were barefooted. Some had wound gaudy scarves about their unkempt hair. Others boasted a profusion of gold and jewellery which Joanna had learned would be given and gambled away in the first sizeable town. They flaunted it here, or perhaps it was the safest way of looking after it.

She said so aloud and Kester reproved her. 'Have you not yet learned of the code of honour among buccaneers? I thought the lessons you witnessed on Hispaniola would have taught you something.'

'What will become of Claris?' she asked abruptly.

'Do you care after what she tried to do to you?'

Joanna's mouth drooped at the corners and for an instant her lips trembled. 'She did not succeed,' she reminded him quietly. 'You made sure of that.'

'I did, indeed, and I have ensured that Claris will have an opportunity to thrive by leaving her within reach of some of her buried booty. She is a resourceful girl. She will survive.'

'I suppose she was once a good maid,' said Joanna in low, bitter tones. 'Why must men always sully virtue?'

The Raven's harsh laugh turned several heads his way. 'Always? Surely not the puritan Matthias . . .!'

Joanna sprang to her feet. 'Oh, you are vile! You judge him by yourself!'

He rose, towering above her, shutting out the sun and hiding her face from his men. 'Have I harmed you, madam?'

She stared at him, inexplicable sadness flowing through her, filling her burning eyes, softening her lovely face. He caught his breath and for a moment his dark eyes assumed a gentle quality. Then there was a yell from the lookout and he became once more the efficient privateer captain, ordering Joanna to the cabin, issuing commands crisply. A sloop carrying a collection of tattered sails and flying a black and white flag was approaching insolently close to the other ship. The brigantine, manoeuvrable with her variety of rigging, circled round and a warning was shouted to the men on the sloop. They were near enough for Joanna, staring through the cabin windows, to see that they were a raggle-taggle collection and that the flag sported a crude piratical device.

A defiant shot was fired from the sloop and was answered immediately by a warning shot across her bows. Again she replied with fire and the next shot from the brigantine landed accurately, sending the mizzen mast crashing to the deck amid screams and drunken yells. Within minutes the brigantine and her sister ship were out of range. The cabin door opened and Kester entered. 'Are you all right? You were not alarmed?'

Joanna realised with surprise that she had felt no fear and knew that her sense of security was engendered by her trust in the Raven. 'Who were they?' she asked.

'Renegade carrion,' he replied. 'They prey upon any who cross their path and kill and maim without mercy.'

Joanna felt suddenly ill. 'Is it always like this in the Caribbean? At home . . .' Her voice faltered as her senses recalled the tranquil atmosphere she had left behind. 'At home,' she repeated, 'we heard of lawlessness and piracy, but it was so remote. I could never have imagined the reality.'

Kester's voice was tauntingly soft. 'Poor Joanna. Flung into so vile a world. Would you have come if you had suspected?'

She stammered, 'M . . . my duty lay in following my . . . obligations.'

'And it has led you here, to the deck of a privateer's vessel.'

She lifted her head, giving him a cool stare. 'Not correct, sir. Your . . . infamy has brought me here.'

The words lay heavily between them and Joanna swallowed hard as irritation spread over his face. 'My so-called infamy rescued you not once, but twice, from defloration by Captain Pryce!'

'I . . . I have never failed to render thanks to you for placing me beyond his reach the first time, but if you had taken me straight to my betrothed I would not have found it necessary to try to escape with Claris.'

She had begun by feeling glad of the opportunity to remind him of her grievance, but her rational tone failed and her sentence ended in a gasp as the Raven stepped close. Again she had an overwhelming sensation of being invaded by his presence. His nearness dominated her and she had to strive not to step back. With a tremendous effort she raised her eyes to look into his. She was unprepared for the blazing passion she saw depicted. She could not decipher its meaning. Hate? Resentment? Desire? A dry sob tore through her. Would she never be delivered from these continual displays of naked emotion?

'Kester,' she said shakily, 'I am truly thankful you found me that first day and for the restraint you have shown me . . .' her mind blacked out the memory of kisses given and returned . . . 'You have absolute power over me—pray, will you not exercise it by releasing me?'

'Do you really wish to leave me, Joanna?'

His words were barely audible and her heart fluttered. Would he take her to New Providence? Perhaps they were already on their way.

'I must go to Matthias,' she insisted.

Slowly his arms came out and slid about her. She should move, she should protest, but the insidious need, the compelling sweetness was taking her over. She raised her lips to his and their kiss was no longer the rapacious plunder of a maid's honour by an unscrupulous predator, but the shared enchantment of two vibrant people.

He drew back his head and gazed down into her moist eyes. Her lips were parted and eager, her arms had slipped around his waist and clung to him. Then with a movement as abrupt as a physical blow he thrust her from him and groaned.

'Is this a new game,' he rasped. 'Do you think to gain your way by clever use of your body?'

He turned from her and strode from the cabin, and as she clung to the table to aid her trembling legs she could hear him yelling orders. She winced at the sharp crack of fist on bone as some foolhardy seaman dared to prevaricate, and wished there was some way to assuage her humiliation at having softened to him and been repulsed.

She awoke the next morning and walked on deck to see that they were approaching an island. Not one of the surf-ringed cays with which these seas abounded, but a substantial place whose blue mountains rose, wreathed with mist, high into the sky. The ships were brought to anchor in a lovely half-moon harbour and Joanna watched the bustling docks with a quickening pulse. For a while she imagined that Kester had brought her to New Providence. She was soon enlightened on her error when he appeared at breakfast, immaculate as always, and announced that he was going ashore.

'What is this place?' she asked breathlessly.

He stared at her between narrowed lids. 'Port Royal, Jamaica,' he said briefly.

Joanna dared not examine her immediate reaction. She shoved her thoughts aside. 'It looks beautiful,' she breathed. 'May I go ashore?'

'You may not!'

She waited for him to enlarge on his brusque refusal and when he did not she asked through suddenly dry lips, 'Why not? Do you intend to cut me off for ever from my fellows?'

He helped himself to bread and spread it with preserve. 'This is as stale as leather,' he grumbled. 'Thank heaven we can obtain civilised supplies here. Jamaica has all a man may need in the way of comfort.'

To her tortured nerves his voice seemed to hold added meaning. 'So you will go ashore and eat and . . . and carouse, while I remain a prisoner.'

'Carouse?' he grinned. 'You are my prisoner, madam, and I do not desire you to be seen.'

'I am not surprised you are ashamed of the way you treat me!'

He laughed. 'This is Jamaica, madam, not your slow little West-country town.'

'Where we are not altogether without enlightenment,' she snapped. 'I know there is law here and a governor, Sir Thomas Modyford, who holds power beneath the king, and he has a lady too. Oh, Kester, please allow me to land.'

He rose abruptly. 'You will remain on board. You will be watched, but there is no jealous woman to assist you this time.'

'I should not be surprised that you fear to parade your crime against me before others,' she sneered.

'You will stay out of sight of folk on the quay,' said the Raven coldly. 'If you are detected in any act of rebellion you will be locked up. I advise you not to provoke any of my seadogs left aboard. They are already resentful of their restriction.'

He was rowed ashore and Joanna watched him through a spyglass as he made his way between the sailors, slaves and pack animals on the bustling quays to disappear towards the town.

Will came to stand by her and she said furiously, 'He will not release me. He will not even allow me to go ashore.'

'Where would you go, mistress?'

'Straight to the governor,' she retorted, 'to ask for succour and help in gaining my destination.'

Will fell silent and Joanna, after gazing longingly at the beauty of the forbidden territory, went back into the cabin and endeavoured to read.

Kester did not return that night and she lay sleepless in the four-poster bed, listening to the sounds which drifted across the bay from the shore, or other ships. Revellers laughed and quarrelled; music unfamiliar and, to her ears, discordant, floated out over the water.

Once she rose and stared through the windows at the many lights. Evidently Jamaica flaunted a thriving night life.

At last, nearing dawn, she managed to get some repose and awoke to another sun-filled day. Boats were rowed from the harbour and stores taken aboard. Will served her with fresh meat and vegetables, pineapples and bananas, clear water and hot chocolate with creamy milk. He explained that much of the provendor came from the governor's estates.

Joanna was startled. 'Surely Captain Venn has not purloined them!'

Will laughed. 'Bless you, no, mistress. They're friends from a long way back. It's Sir Thomas Modyford who gives him his letter of marque, on behalf of His Majesty, of course.'

'Who does not understand that it enables fearful crimes to be perpetrated in his name,' said Joanna coldly. 'Does the noble governor of Jamaica have any idea that he is abetting murderers and thieves?'

Will refused to be riled. He scratched his grey head and grinned. 'From all I hear of King Charles he's too clever a fellow to be ignorant of what happens out here. As for Sir Thomas—well, he's a realist. He knows that the British couldn't stay in the Caribbean if they didn't have the friendship and protection of the privateers. There's too many vagabonds who'd destroy them.'

'A fine excuse for licentiousness and piracy,' scorned Joanna, 'and a false one, for there are those who extract a living from the islands without resorting to crime.'

Will gave her a sidelong glance as she continued, 'You may not know that I was on my way to my betrothed on New Providence when I was captured. Master Kemp wrote letters to say that he has made a home for me in which I hoped—still hope—to enjoy a peaceful married life.'

Will's mouth opened and closed, then he shook his head helplessly. Joanna was not surprised that he could not find further words to defend his master. She finished the last of the tiny sweet bananas appreciatively and ate some pineapple. She had once tasted the latter at the home of a wealthy acquaintance, but bananas were new to her. She drank deeply of the sweet, cool water which had been carried aboard especially for her.

It was dusky outside and soon in the abrupt way to which she had grown accustomed the tropic night would descend. She walked on deck, invisible now from the dock, and raised her head to catch the delectable breezes blowing off shore.

A boat approached swiftly and she was not quick enough to suppress the delight she felt at realising Kester was returning. He looked displeased as he climbed aboard and she was disappointed. Apparently he had no wish to see her and she wondered what had dragged him from the immoderate pleasures of the flesh which Jamaica undoubtedly had to offer a man of good appearance and rich substance.

He jerked his head towards the cabin. 'Inside at once,' he ordered. 'I must speak to you.'

Resentment flooded through her. He had brought her to an enchanting looking island which he forced her to view from a distance and now he returned after many hours of enjoyment and spoke to her like a slave. But she *was* a slave! As she stared into his enigmatic dark eyes she had the feeling that he read her thoughts. His face was grim, his attitude unbending, and she sped into the cabin.

He gave a small bow. 'I regret to inform you that you must go below at once and stay there.'

She gasped. Below meant the tiny cabin she supposed. She felt her panic returning. Trying to keep an even voice she begged, 'Please do not shut me up again. I . . . I find the idea unbearable.'

'You *must* go below,' he said inexorably. 'I have no choice but to conceal you.'

Her eyes widened. 'Why? What possible reason can you have?'

'Lady Modyford has decided that she would like to take dinner aboard. She has some romantic notion that it would be amusing to eat on a privateer. Of course, it is cooler out on the water. Perhaps that is why . . .'

Joanna threw back her head in a scornful laugh. 'I see! So although you profess to scorn convention, and buy me as your property, you are not man enough to allow your grand friends to find you out.'

She had forgotten his blazing rages and she trembled inwardly as he took a step nearer. 'Damn you for an argumentative female. I am not ashamed of anything I have done. I am concerned for your welfare—your reputation.'

Joanna's mouth opened. 'You cannot be serious! You
drag me about the oceans with you, parade me before
scurvy buccaneers as your possession, refuse to allow me
to pursue my respectable alliance, and now you pretend
to care about my reputation. What have I left, sir, that
could be damaged?'

'A great deal, madam,' he grated. 'I have dealt le-
niently with you, but if you continue to anger me . . .'
He stopped, passing a lean brown hand across his face.
'Joanna, pray do not argue with me. I do not wish to
jeopardise your future beyond hope by giving the
Modyfords an untrue picture of you.'

'You can scarcely expect me to believe *that*! You are
afraid—and correctly so—that I would appeal to the
governor who would surely order my release.'

'I am afraid of no such thing, madam, and you will
walk below or be carried.'

She lifted her head. 'It seems I have no choice—as
usual.'

Rebelliously Joanna followed Will to the tiny windowless cabin below decks and clenched her hands as she
entered. Will turned in the doorway. 'Mistress Seldon—
I hate to lock you in—if you swear not to come above
decks while the guests are here . . .' Depressed at the
prospect of a locked cabin, grateful for Will's lenience,
she gave her word and relinquished the hope of an
appeal to the governor. When Will had gone she tried to
read. It was impossible and she found her uncom-
prehending eyes were going over the same verses. She
put the poetry away and picked up the Bible, turning to
the fly leaf, pondering on the boy whose life had been
ruined by murder and rapine and slavery. No wonder he
was sealed in bitterness. Yet surely no man was ir-
reclaimable. Unbidden, her mind roved over the memory of his kisses, his occasional gentleness, his rare
smile. What a wonderful husband he could make, so
strong and courageous and clever. She paced the floor,

but could not escape her wanton imaginings and the walls of the cabin seemed to close in on her, bringing perspiration pouring down her body, tightening her throat to suffocation.

She could not stay in the cabin. She had heard the arrival of the Modyfords ages ago and felt that by now they must be lingering over the last of their meal. Surely there could be no harm in walking the narrow deck below, anywhere to escape for a moment from the terror.

She opened the door and her breathing eased. She would walk just a few steps to the foot of the gangway where she could look up at the stars. She saw them, enormous in the velvety blackness, and drew in deep breaths of refreshing air. A lamp burned above her head, swinging to and fro in the gentle harbour swell. Then the sky was blotted out by a figure.

Joanna could not make out a face, but the words were perfectly clear. 'Sir Christopher, you are a sly dog. You have a new female below.'

A man's voice, now followed by a woman's, '*Not* the pretty Claris? Have you a different companion?'

Joanna was frozen in shock. Kester had been absolutely correct in predicting that his guests would think only evil of her and she had defeated his attempt to conceal her presence aboard. She had also betrayed her promise to Will.

Her brain seethed with conflicting courses of action. Perhaps she should grasp the chance of revealing herself completely to the governor and his lady in the hope that they would put a better interpretation on her position. But they were friends of Kester's and, presumably, other privateers, so maybe they would choose not to believe her. And if they did could Kester be prosecuted for abduction? She did not want him harmed.

Her indecision held her fast and the woman looked down at Joanna's face, clearly illumined beneath a lamp.

'What a lovely creature!'

Her tone was condescendingly amused and Joanna panicked and ran back to the cabin, hurling the door shut behind her.

She waited, wondering what Kester would do. Were they discussing her and laughing? At last she heard the sound of the guests departing and almost immediately Kester opened the door to the cabin. He had been drinking and the fumes of rum and brandy floated in with him. He was flushed, but still immaculate. Tonight he wore black breeches, but had so far yielded to fashion as to permit himself a coat of claret-coloured watered silk, with a cravat of finest lawn and Venetian lace ruffles at his wrists. On his fingers were rings of gold and diamonds and there were more diamonds in his shoe buckles.

He gave her no time to admire. His voice was as abrasive as his face was grim. 'So! Through Will's mistaken indulgence and your untrustworthy betrayal the Modyfords have had a clear sight of you.'

Joanna had been about to express regret in spite of her deep resentment at the entire episode, but his aggressive fury angered her. She just failed to make her shrug careless, but it incensed him all the same and he gestured to the door and strode away, clearly expecting her to follow.

She ached to defy him, but her need to get out on deck outweighed her resistance and he must know this. It made her even more enraged.

In the great cabin he waved away men who were clearing the remains of a feast. 'Now, madam, you have landed us in a fine pickle.'

'I sought air! If you had been forced to occupy that ghastly cabin you would understand what it is to be helpless and . . .'

She stopped, recalling his frightful past, and he gave a wolfish grin. 'Exactly, madam, you need never remind me what such a sensation is like.'

'No! Well, it makes your behaviour all the more reprehensible. Why do you deal so with me?'

'Why do you think I did it?'

She was taken aback. 'You had a reason other than . . . than a wish to vent your revenge on a . . . Puritan?'

His eyes were fixed on her in a way which made her heart beat with a slow, heavy pounding as he said, 'I have thought of little but you lately, Joanna.'

He walked to the window and began to tap a pane with one fingernail and she was breathless as she waited. Then he turned. 'We sail at dawn.'

She was bewildered. Of the various courses of action he might take it had not occurred to her that he would remove her from Jamaica without now giving her an opportunity to meet the Modyfords, and endeavour to explain her true position to them.

Her cheeks paled. 'I wonder you brought me here at all. You have no intention of reuniting me with civilised folk.'

His voice was coldly even. 'I am here to hand over the government's share of the latest booty. I pay ten per cent of all I take to the King's House.'

Joanna said angrily, 'I am sure that the people in Britain can have no knowledge of such perfidy.'

'You are a babe in these matters. I wonder at your father allowing you to come into the world with so little comprehension.'

'My father could never dream of the crimes committed in these islands in the name of the good folk of Britain.'

The Raven smiled thinly. 'Could he not? Well, I do not care one way or the other.'

'You care for nothing!' she burst out, goaded by her sick frustration. He was going to sail out again into the deep Caribbean waters to pursue his piratical course, not even permitting her to tread the ivory white beaches of Jamaica, or stroll in the tempting green forests.

Before she could voice her indignation the Raven spoke again. 'I was pushed into a lie on your behalf. I told the Modyfords that I picked you up after your vessel had been so damaged by gales that you alone had survived. I wanted no mention made of Pryce's name. I said that you had been extremely ill as a result of your privations and that you were too mortified to come into company until you had assumed your rightful place in society.'

'What utter nonsense! Surely they did not believe you. As if I would be so wishy-washy.'

Real amusement flickered over his face. 'I know that, but they do not. I fear I was forced to depict you as a die-away young woman with an excess of sensibility. However, you can tell any tale you like once . . . once I have undone the wrong I have perpetrated.'

'What do you mean?'

Kester turned to stare out to sea. 'I now deplore my treatment of you. I intend to sail at once for New Providence and deliver you to your betrothed, which is what I should have done in the first place. He will believe the somewhat irregular story you will need to concoct if he loves you as . . . as he ought.'

He swung round abruptly to look into her eyes and Joanna felt as if he was dragging up her soul to meet his. A voice of protest screamed inside her, and died, as he bowed deeply and walked from the cabin, not looking behind him, and closed the door.

CHAPTER
SEVEN

THE brigantine sailed from the bay as the sun tipped the palms with red-gold. Joanna leaned on the deck rail watching as the blue mountains finally faded from view. She was going to Matthias at last and she should be happy at the prospect, and grateful to the Raven who had decided to behave with honour.

But try as she might she could not find any joy in her situation. If only her original voyage had not been interrupted, she would by now be wed and settled and her mind and body would not be harassed by visions of a different man—a different life.

It would be all right once Kester had deposited her on New Providence and sailed away. Of course it would. He joined her at the rail and she greeted him briefly. He looked bronzed and powerful, his dark hair bare in the strong sun, his white shirt open at the neck.

'You should be wearing your hat,' he said.

'I have grown to like the sun on my face.'

'Your future husband may not appreciate the colour of your skin. He will expect to receive you as he left you—a woman with a complexion as white as her soul.'

'You take a delight in mocking me, sir.'

He was unexpectedly solemn. 'I do not mock you, my dear. Rather I mock myself for my forgetfulness of women of innocence and purity.'

'Do not place me on a pedestal,' gasped Joanna, feeling a surge of shame as she realised that she preferred him to see her as a woman ripe for caresses.

She turned away, afraid she might reveal her thoughts, and stared at the spume in their wake. 'I daresay Matthias will accept my appearance without question after my time at sea, and in any case the sunburn will soon fade.'

'No doubt he will dress you in black and other sombre colours and never appreciate the glory of the golden girl you have become.'

He sounded bitter and Joanna remained silent. He straightened. 'Come with me. I have brought you something from Jamaica.'

In the main cabin Joanna watched Will and Kester carry in bundles which they untied to reveal quantities of stuffs. She gave cries of delight at the crimsons and blues, the greens and yellows. Her fingers explored the softness of satin and muslin and velvet. She knelt at a box and lifted out shoes of finest kid and gloves of perfumed cotton and leather, fans of feathers and lace, shawls of delicate wool and shimmering silk.

'They will be of no use to you, after all,' said Kester gloomily, 'but I could not resist showing you what I purchased before I made my decision.'

'You *purchased* them?'

'I paid proper market prices. I know you hate wearing captured gowns, especially . . .' he paused and a faint colour came into his face, '. . . of the kind not intended for a young maid. I hoped you would find pleasure in sewing garments of lovely colours in styles more fitted to your modesty.'

'What a pleasing idea!' exclaimed Joanna. 'Oh, how I would like to wear them. I fear I am often not a good Puritan at heart.'

Kester leaned forward, his arm brushing hers, to pick up a length of tobacco brown silk and another of pearl grey. 'Would your man object to these?'

'I do not know. I hope not, for I intend to have them!'

She found scissors, thimbles, needles and thread and was vociferous in her surprise that he should have known exactly what to purchase.

He looked a trifle sheepish. 'Lady Modyford helped

me. Elizabeth was horrified when she realised you had been using garments intended for . . . a different sort of woman. She asked me also to tell you that when you have settled on New Providence to your satisfaction she would welcome you and . . . your husband as guests.'

'She sounds nice, though I do not think Matthias will find much in common with the governor or his lady.' She sighed gently and Kester glanced at her and said quickly, 'Er . . . Elizabeth insisted on one other . . . comfort for you.'

He left the cabin and returned a moment later pushing a girl before him. She showed evidence of many races in her features which were the brown of the Indian. Her hair was short and curly like an African, but her hazel eyes betrayed a white forebear. Joanna stared at her and she looked down at her shuffling feet.

'Lady Modyford sent me a girl!'

'She thought it scandalous that you had no maid,' explained Kester. 'The wench is from her own household, well trained and skilled with her needle.'

Joanna said softly to the slender girl in her dun coloured gown, 'What is your name?'

'If you please, mistress, it's Lovejoy.'

Joanna almost choked. 'L . . . Lovejoy? And will you be happy to come with me to New Providence. Life there may not be as easy as it has been with your former mistress, and it could be long before I can send you back to visit your family. Will you mind very much?'

Lovejoy's eyes opened wide. 'Family? Lor', mistress, I ain't got a family. I was only a child when I was bought.'

'Bought! Kester, is this girl a *slave*?'

He answered evenly, 'What do you expect? There are no freeborn servants on the islands.'

'I cannot own a slave,' stated Joanna flatly. 'It is against all the precepts of my beliefs.'

Lovejoy understood only that the beautiful lady found

her unpleasing. Her liquid eyes filled with tears. 'Don't
send me back. Lady Modyford will think I was disobe-
dient and have me beat.'

'She *beats* her slaves?'

'Only when we're very bad, mistress, and often times
she forgives us and she don't do it herself, not like some,
and she don't allow us to be beat very hard.'

Joanna said coldly to Kester, 'I wish you had introduced me to the girl before we sailed. You must find a
way of returning Lovejoy to her mistress.'

'I explained that she is already sold to me. If you send
her back she may be purchased by a very different kind
of owner. In any case, you need someone to help with
the stitching and it is unseemly not to have a maid with
you in case you are unwell.'

Joanna's exclamation of indignation broke on a shaky
laugh. 'Not seemly! After all that has occurred . . .!'

His voice was glacial. 'I desire you to keep the wench
by you, madam. You have no choice in the matter until I
deliver you to Master Kemp.'

The rebuff was like a douche of cold water. Joanna
had almost forgotten her status. 'I see,' she said causti-
cally, 'a slave to serve a slave!' She curtseyed low. 'Very
well, *Master*, if it be your command, Lovejoy may
stay.'

The slave, who could not have been above fifteen,
understood that she was accepted, and her life had led
her to be uncritical. She did not expect appreciation. She
cried out with delight over the brilliant stuffs and set to at
once with measuring line and scissors. Joanna told her to
begin on the brown and had not the heart to explain that
her future master would never allow the wearing of the
bright silks.

By the time they reached New Providence the two
women had fashioned a gown which was pretty, but
modest, with a white tucker at the throat and long
sleeves. Kester viewed it without enthusiasm.

'Beauty such as yours should be enhanced, not con-cealed,' he said, but it was his only comment and Joanna struggled with disappointment. On the short voyage he had maintained a distance between them, even though taking his meals with her and sleeping in the day cabin, but his courtesy had been of the kind he would extend to any unknown lady passenger and Joanna had lain sleep-less in the fourposter bed, trying not to think of him lying so near, endeavouring to decide how she would conduct life with Matthias.

They waited for daybreak before entering the harbour and she looked anxiously at her future home. It was not in the least bit like Jamaica. The beaches were as white and the palms waved as gently in the azure sky, but the dwellings on shore were insubstantial and there was an array of ragged tents to one side of the harbour. As they negotiated the reefs she realised they were closely watched by men who lay among the high coral which ringed the busy waters.

Kester was watching her face as he said, 'I hope that Master Kemp is strong, for New Providence has become increasingly a haven for pirates.'

The revelation was admittedly not so great a shock to her as if she had sailed straight here from England, but her disappointment, allied to inner turmoil, made her sharp. 'You should feel at home here!'

She held her breath but he failed to rise to the challenge, leaning on the wooden rail, staring at the shore, while behind him the bo'sun shouted an order to drop anchor.

The black and white flag had been replaced by the simple Cross of St George and only a limited number of men, respectably garbed, were on view, the others hav-ing been commanded to remain out of sight. The ship, as always, was spotlessly clean and in perfect order and looked far neater than many of the craft lying at anchor. In fact, several of the vessels were unsalubrious, cluttered, with unswabbed decks and neglected sails.

'It is not like I imagined—and hoped,' said Joanna hesitantly to Kester.

He shrugged powerful shoulders. 'There is a small colony which endeavours to pursue a peaceful existence, though it cannot be easy for them.'

'It is never easy to live a good life!' Joanna sounded as disheartened as she felt. 'I thought—and so did Matthias—that the Indies would be a new beginning for us.'

His voice was rough. 'And why should it not? You show little patience! Perhaps your betrothed has a splendid dwelling awaiting you.'

She bit her lip, finding her feeling of desolation impossible to shake off. A messenger was despatched bearing a letter from her to Matthias. She had given much thought to its composition during the voyage and finally had explained to him that the merchant ship had been attacked by dastardly pirates and vagabonds, but that a gentleman had come to her aid and brought her safely to shore. She accounted for the time taken by the fact that Captain Venn had been carrying possessions due to the crown and had been compelled to visit Jamaica first. The explanation was a mixture of truth and disemblance. She regretted beginning her new life with deception, but she could see no other course open to her. And after all, she was innocent of wrongdoing and as pure as when she left England. She stifled the voice which tried to tell her that she no way resembled the Puritan maid who had waited at home for her betrothed to send for her.

Joanna awaited the return of the messenger, leaning on the deck rail, while Kester went into the cabin and closed the door. The gesture seemed symbolic of their approaching parting. When the black clad figure appeared on the dock waving her letter, she felt her knees turn to water. She called faintly and Kester joined her in a rowboat which took her ashore. She stepped onto the

harbour and greeted her betrothed who took both her
hands in his in an usually open gesture before pressing
his narrow lips to her forehead.

'Let us thank God for your safe arrival,' he said. 'As
soon as you are installed with a neighbour's wife we shall
go to the Meeting House.'

Joanna fought with a sense of depression which
shamed her. She had forgotten how slight in stature he
was, scarcely taller than she, and surely he was thinner
than she recalled. But his eyes were kind and his
welcome genuine.

He gave a small correct bow to Kester. 'I give you my
humble gratitude, Captain Venn, for your part in her
rescue. Pray, will you take a meal with us?'

Kester returned the bow. 'I thank you, sir, but my
business compels me to sail on the next tide.'

Joanna sensed her betrothed's relief. The captain's
clothes might be black, but the exquisite lace and costly
jewellery betrayed the fact that he had little in common
with Puritans. Joanna felt almost sick with disappointment. She knew they had to part, but the moment was
upon her too soon. Was he really going immediately? A
brief word, a bow, and never to meet again except
perhaps as distant acquaintances. She felt she could not
endure it.

Lovejoy moved closer and drew Matthias's attention.
His nose twitched slightly in disapproval. 'Is this your
maid?'

When Joanna had asked Kester if Lovejoy would
betray him to Master Kemp as a privateer he had
laughed. 'She knows me as a gentleman who visits her
master.'

Lovejoy's eyes were solemn as she regarded the crow-
like figure of her mistress's future husband. She bobbed
a curtsey, her long lashes drooping over her eyes, and
Matthias gave her a suspicious stare before he gestured
to her to pick up Joanna's bundle.

He spoke to Kester. 'Pray, sir, give me the reckoning for replacing Mistress Seldon's garments.'

Joanna held her breath. She had brought as little as possible, restraining herself to a few personal items and the grey cloth and she expected Kester's rapier-like tongue to produce a wounding reply to what surely he would consider a presumptuous demand, but he said mildly, 'The few items can be a bride gift. I beg you to accept them.'

Matthias looked slightly displeased, but he bowed and nodded and Joanna was embarrassed by his ungracious reaction. She glanced at Kester to find his eyes softer than she had ever seen them. He seemed to understand and sympathise. He always understood! The anguish of sudden self-knowledge twisted her heart and quailed her spirit. *I love Him*! she thought, *I love him, and I always will*! Dear God, why had she to discover such a truth? Why now? If she had realised before she might have prevailed upon Kester to allow her to stay with him. If she had *never* realised the truth she might have found a measure of contentment with Matthias. He stood waiting for her, watching her with expectant eyes. She looked again at Kester, wondering what she would do if, even now, he begged her to stay with him, and knew she would toss aside the teachings of a lifetime and follow him for ever. But he gave her only a murmured farewell. Did his dark eyes express more? Regret? Maybe so, but perhaps only at his failure to possess her.

She drew a shuddering breath and sank before him in a curtsey, the depth of which tightened Matthias's lips in disapproval. Puritan ladies left such displays to their royalist sisters. Then with shocking abruptness Matthias was leading her away, away from the harbour and the *Lady Margaret*, along a rough track between trees, and she dared not look back.

The jungle closed about them, the enormous trees blocking out the sunlight. The smells, sights, sounds, were similar to those on Hispaniola, but the company was different, very different.

Matthias said in a tight voice. 'You have been beset by many perils, Joanna. I am heartily thankful that you survived unscathed.'

She was scarcely able to articulate. She was far from unscathed, but her wounds could never be displayed and would never heal.

'Captain Venn brought an invitation for us to visit Sir Thomas and Lady Modyford,' said Matthias. 'Is her ladyship a seemly woman of the kind your late mother would have approved?'

'I . . . I did not meet her,' faltered Joanna.

Matthias threw her an astonished look. 'Yet you were on Jamaica and she found you a maid.'

Lovejoy was dawdling several yards behind and could not hear and Joanna said, 'I preferred to remain aboard ship. I felt my position to be somewhat ambiguous.'

'I see,' said Matthias, though he looked a little sceptical. 'Well, once you hold a position as my wife you need fear no one's scrutiny.'

They walked deeper into the forest and she was weighed down by the breathless humidity. Then there was a flash of blue-green and she exclaimed, 'A hummingbird just like the one I saw . . .' She stopped, enveloped in chagrin.

Matthias gave her a suspicious sideways glance. 'When did you see such a bird? Before today you have not trod one of these islands.'

'I . . . I borrowed a spyglass from Captain Venn.' She must guard her tongue or she might reveal more of her history, and she had not so far told any lies exactly.

They reached a clearing in which there were several dwellings. They were not large and were shaped quite roughly in stone and wood, each with a patch of ground behind walls where there were dark-skinned workers.

Matthias threw open a gate. 'This is our home. It is not

as you have been used to, but time will increase our prosperity, I do not doubt.'

As they walked up the narrow driveway the toiling servants straightened their backs to stare. Matthias muttered, 'Lazy good-for-nothings. They know not the meaning of hard work.'

'Are they native to the island?' asked Joanna.

Matthias's thin cheeks coloured. 'They were brought in and I was forced to purchase them.'

'Slaves! You keep slaves!'

'Certainly not! To obtain labour one must buy human beings, but I have freed them. Unfortunately, as free men and women they work only when they need to eat or drink. It all keeps us Puritans poorer than ever.'

Inside the house Joanna strove not to feel disheartened. The furniture had been carpentered from local wood and inexpertly put together and was scarcely planed smooth and certainly not polished. The windows were tiny, the price of glass being extortionate in the islands, explained Matthias, and the drapes were of cheap cotton. She found it difficult to view the place dispassionately, or as she might have done had she not been shown a more luxurious way of life. Sudden shame flooded her and impulsively she leaned forward and kissed Matthias's cheek. He drew back as if she had been a snake.

'Joanna! Such immoderation! It will be soon enough when we are wed and even then . . .'

Her heart grew leaden. She had forgotten his lack of humour, his correctness which even her father had found daunting at times. She cast her eyes down in the way of a Puritan maid and murmured an apology for her boldness, but she heard nothing of his stilted speech of forgiveness, lost in remembrances of the strong arms, the searching kisses of a privateer.

She was dragged back from her reverie by the entrance of a small bustling woman whom she liked immediately. 'I am Mistress Abigail Jones. I hope we shall be friends.'

Joanna felt she could make a friend of the young, sweet-faced girl who was far gone with child, but she was nervous of her companion. Mistress Gisburn was thin faced and sour looking. She was a widow, though still fairly young, and Joanna fancied she detected a proprietorial attitude towards Matthias and a resentful one towards herself.

Mistress Gisburn allowed her cold eyes to travel over Joanna's gown. 'My how grand you are! Such rich silk will not do for life here. Master Kemp needs a working wife who will not scorn to soil her hands.'

Matthias frowned. 'Mistress Seldon has been through much. She lost everything and was kindly helped by Lady Modyford of Jamaica. We must procure some good, hard-wearing cloth and she can fashion a proper sort of garment and the silk can be given away.'

Not if I can help it, vowed Joanna. The tobacco brown silk was her only link with Raven. Besides, she had grown to like the feel of soft clothes, but she said nothing, while Abigail Jones stifled a nervous giggle.

Mistress Gisburn had come to remove Joanna to her own home where she was to reside until the wedding. Her house contained more in the way of possessions. Apparently her late husband had been quite successful and she had been left comfortable when he died of a fever.

Joanna was shown to a small apartment containing a narrow bed covered by a white quilt. There were white curtains moving lazily in the breeze and a marble-topped stand holding white china. A plain deal clothes press stood beside a table on which lay a Bible. The room was without comfort or character and Joanna's thoughts fled to the cabin on the *Lady Margaret* with its enormous fourposter bed with the soft mattress and rich hangings. She stepped forward and felt the bed, more in order to relieve her feelings than in any need to discover the quality of the mattress.

Mistress Gisburn said quickly, 'It's hard all right! You'll not find any sinful luxuries in my abode. I believe in reasonable living and no more.'

Joanna did not answer and when she was bidden to the dinner table she seated herself opposite Matthias who seemed very much at home here and ate roast suckling pig with split peas, baked fish and spices sparingly, as always, masticating his food meticulously and laying down his knife between bites. He seldom looked up and the meal was conducted almost in silence while Mistress Gisburn waited on him with anticipatory care. Joanna was left in no doubt that if she had never turned up her hostess would have been well pleased. She could eat little, although she managed to enjoy pineapples and oranges at the end of the meal.

She was surprised to see Matthias light up a pipe. He coloured faintly as he said, 'I trust you do not object, Joanna. Tobacco is a great comfort to a man in this wild place.'

Giving Joanna no time to answer Mistress Gisburn intervened, 'Why should she object? New Providence is bad enough for a woman, but for a man making his living it is exceedingly hard.'

Joanna bit back a retort that she did not require such instruction. She was going to find life here difficult enough without antagonising the womenfolk, but her heart quailed at the idea of spending her life with Matthias beneath the watchful gaze of Mistress Gisburn and others like her.

The servants had cleared away and they were drinking a dish of tea when the senior maid burst into the room. 'Oh, Mistress Gisburn, there's a woman come from Mistress Jones's house. She's been taken terrible ill— the midwives don't know what to do. They say she and the baby will die soon.'

Mistress Gisburn drew back her head. 'How dare you come into the room in so immoderate a manner and blurt such things out before Master Kemp! Are we physicians or surgeons? What can we do?'

The maid talked rapidly, 'I know you can't help, ma'am, but she's suffering dreadfully. Her husband is in despair—he sees himself left with no wife and four little ones to look after.'

'If it is God's will . . .' intoned Matthias.

'Exactly so,' agreed Mistress Gisburn.

The maid turned to Joanna. 'They were wondering if there's a medical man aboard the ship that brought you, Mistress Seldon. She hasn't sailed yet. Our own died of a coughing sickness months ago. Is there anyone who can help poor Mistress Jones?'

Joanna hesitated, thinking of Robert Jennison. He might be dead drunk; he might have no understanding of a childbed, or no inclination to involve himself. Yet if there was a chance of helping Abigail Jones . . . 'There is someone on board the *Lady Margaret*,' she said, 'though he is frequently . . . ill. You can certainly try.'

The maid ran out and moments later they heard the messenger race down the path. Mistress Gisburn pressed her lips together. 'We must pray for Mistress Jones tonight,' and Matthias nodded solemnly.

Joanna felt stifled. 'I should like to walk outside,' she gasped.

They stared at her. 'It is unwise in the heat of noon,' explained Mistress Gisburn. 'Even the men leave out-door work to the overseers until evening.'

A picture of Kester, bronzed and heedless of the burning sun crossed Joanna's mind and she closed her eyes, fighting back tears.

Matthias said not unkindly, 'My dear, you have suffered much. Will you not retire and rest. I know Mistress Gisburn will not object.'

Her hostess clearly did not care for the suggestion. 'I

intended to instruct Mistress Seldon in the ways of the island community, but I suppose it can wait.'

Joanna fled to the small impersonal bedchamber. She lay on the hard bed and closed her eyes, but the strong sunlight was little held back by the white curtains and the light beat back at her from the stark walls. She rose and stared through the small window at servants who dawdled away the afternoon in the garden while a man whom she presumed to be the overseer lounged in the shelter of a tree and smoked. Even Mistress Gisburn appeared to have insufficient command over her servants. Kester Venn would not have brooked such insubordination. She checked the thought. He must not be allowed to infiltrate her mind. She tried hard to visualise herself the chatelaine of a similar estate, spending her days coping with irresponsible servants, checking household supplies, caring for livestock, and her nights . . . her mind jumped immediately aside from Matthias into a dream in which she lay with the man she loved. She pressed her hands to her cheeks, striving for control, and gradually induced a calm resolution. She would put all thoughts of Kester Venn away from her forever. Matthias was a good man who had done nothing to deserve a woman who was faithless, even in thought, and she would marry him and be a good and loving wife.

There was a gentle tap on the door and Lovejoy entered, her eyes large with wonder. 'This is a queer place,' she whispered, 'not a bit like Jamaica. Lady Modyford would have the hide of the lazy, good-for-nothing slaves here.'

'They are free men and women,' explained Joanna.

'Free to do nothing,' giggled Lovejoy. 'I came to tell you that a servant brought a message. They got hold of Master Jennison and he went to the woman in labour.'

'Is there hope for her?'

Lovejoy shrugged. 'They didn't know yet. Women walk a hard road, don't they?'

She left and Joanna lay down again. The air was growing a little cooler and she slipped into a light doze from which she was awakened by the certainty that she was being watched. She lifted her lids to see Mistress Gisburn, her eyes fixed on her with a cold expression of triumph which filled her with apprehension.

CHAPTER
EIGHT

JOANNA sat up, swinging her feet to the floor.

Mistress Gisburn said in a clipped voice, 'Abigail and her baby are saved.' She ignored Joanna's expression of relief and continued, 'The physician was not at all the kind of man I respect. He looked dissipated and his breath smelled of drink.'

Joanna remained silent and Mistress Gisburn said, slowly, 'Of course, *now* I am not surprised by him and I am sure you know well the kind of man he is.'

'I know he has an unfortunate weakness,' replied Joanna evenly. 'I am glad he was skilful enough to save Mistress Jones and the babe.'

'Unfortunate weakness, you call it? But hardly noticeable on the *Lady Margaret*, eh?'

Joanna was alarmed, but said calmly, 'You speak in riddles, ma'am.'

'Then let me be explicit. While the ship was held up some of the seamen slipped ashore. It appears that there were many more men below decks of whom we knew nothing. The gallant captain tried to conceal them, it seems.' After staring watchfully for a few moments Mistress Gisburn slipped away and Joanna slumped, her heart beating hard. Shortly afterwards Lovejoy arrived with a message that Master Kemp desired to speak with her.

She conducted Joanna to a tiny parlour which gave the overall impression of darkness, with heavy oak furniture which must have been brought from Europe, a black fur rug and brown drapes. Matthias was waiting. He turned and a muted shaft of dusty sunlight fell on his features, emphasising the bony structure until it closely resembled a skull. He stared at her for what seemed an age, without speaking.

Her legs felt weak and she asked, 'May we not be seated?'

His voice filled the room. 'You lied to me!'

His harsh words seemed to beat about her head. 'In . . . in what way am I supposed to have lied, Matthias?'

'God alone knows! Now you will please be honest with me and tell me the truth. While the *Lady Margaret* lay at anchor disreputable men came ashore. They are of the kind of whom New Providence has had all too many. Pirates! Buccaneers! The scum of the oceans.'

'Seamen are notoriously rough and dissolute,' said Joanna through lips which would scarcely move.

He gave an angry gesture. 'These men lost no time in getting drunk and told the local whores a pretty tale of a gentlewoman taken from one pirate by another, sold in a market place . . .'

'It is not like it seems!' she cried, 'and Captain Venn is a privateer and a gentleman.'

'So, madam, you had the audacity to come to me knowing that he is a graceless villain and attempt to deceive me with a string of lies!'

'It is not like that, Matthias. He treated me with kindness—he saved me . . .'

'The *Raven*! I did not associate the name Venn with that wicked, evil pirate. How amusing it must all seem to you. Did you laugh together when he acted the part of gentleman to hoodwink me?'

Joanna's words of repudiation and anger died as she realised that Matthias was deeply hurt and humiliated. She said gently, 'We had no desire to hurt you. Far from it. Our only wish was to protect you from any false impression you might have gained.'

'False impression! I had a fleeting doubt when I heard

the story of going to Jamaica with bounty for the king, but this . . .! How long did you remain with the Raven—and in what capacity?'

Joanna's temper flared, 'In the capacity—as you phrase it—of a passenger. I have received only honourable treatment . . .' She stopped, recalling the feel of Kester's mouth searching hers, and her senses flooded with sudden need of him.

Matthias peered at her. 'Are you speaking the absolute truth? Would you swear on God's holy word that you do not lie?'

'If you force me, yes!' cried Joanna, 'though I pray you will not. I desire you to accept my word. Without trust how can our marriage succeed?'

The door opened and Mistress Gisburn came in. 'Do not believe her, Matthias. Make her swear on the Bible. Even she will not dare to blaspheme.'

'You have been listening,' accused Joanna. 'You are infamous!'

'*I* am infamous! What of you? You spend days and nights the only woman on board a pirate vessel, you lie blatantly to your betrothed, as godly a man as ever lived, and you expect us to take you at your word.'

Joanna said quietly, 'I am as pure a maid as when I left my father's house.'

Mistress Gisburn's thin lips smiled knowingly. 'So you say, and if Master Kemp discovers otherwise when he beds you after marriage it will be too late. Once married, there is no going back.'

Joanna gasped and even Matthias put out his hands in protest, but Mistress Gisburn went on relentlessly, 'I make no apology for plain speaking. A maid's virginity is precious beyond rubies. If you are to wed good Master Kemp I feel it is incumbent upon you to allow me, along with other good matrons, to examine you and ascertain your maiden state—or otherwise.'

Joanna went white. 'How dare you! You disgust me!

Rather than submit I would embark on the next ship to England and return to my father.'

Mistress Gisburn's manner was implacable. 'I do not doubt it, madam.'

Joanna turned to Matthias. 'You allow me to be insulted. Is this the kind of treatment your future wife should expect?'

He looked from one woman to the other and Joanna felt a quick contempt for his weakness. 'A man has to be careful. Surely it could not be considered unseemly for the matrons to reassure themselves,' he said, pleadingly.

His vaccillation acted on Joanna like a spur. 'Never!' she cried. 'Never would I permit such an . . . an obscenity.'

Matthias's narrow cheeks flushed. 'Your reluctance is bound to cause me doubt. Mistress Gisburn . . .'

'Is evil minded and salacious,' cried Joanna.

'Such words are unseemly on the lips of a young girl,' pronounced Mistress Gisburn.

Joanna's anger settled in white ice. 'Our betrothal is at an end. I will go to Mistress Jones's house. She will surely not refuse me shelter.'

Mistress Gisburn's lips parted in a jeering laugh. 'Do you propose to burden Abigail Jones when she has just had a difficult birth? What selfishness, to be sure.'

Joanna looked at Matthias, uncertainty and doubt clearly expressed on her open face. She said brokenly, 'I . . . I would not be a nuisance to her. I daresay she would be glad if I offered my services to her as . . . as a maid. I shall go back to England as soon as I can.'

Matthias gave her a studied look which encompassed her tall, slender form, the deep blue of her large, brilliant eyes emphasised by her gentle tan, her hair a glory of shining gold, and all the man in him protested against losing her. Yet even now he did not address her directly. He turned to Mistress Gisburn. 'Forgiveness may be offered for sin truly repented,' he cajoled.

Mistress Gisburn drew back her head to administer another reproof, but Joanna, outrage consuming her, forestalled her, 'I want no forgiveness for sin I have not committed!'

She rushed from the room. She would go to Abigail Jones and make herself useful there until she could go back to her father. Her throat ached and her eyes were filled with blinding tears. She failed to notice the tall figure standing in the dim passage. But as she blundered into it her senses told her whose hands had reached out to assist her.

'Kester,' she gasped, all inhibitions lost in her despair. 'They have said terrible things to me.'

Without a word he gathered her into his arms and carried her from the house, striding down the long path to the dusty road, holding her so tightly she could feel the beating of his heart.

'Put me down,' she begged, shakily, 'What on earth will folk think?'

For a moment he held her, gazing down at her face, then he set her on her feet and she brushed her gown with her hands in an endeavour to hide her confusion.

She mentioned all the things she had left behind, but Kester shrugged aside such minor considerations. 'You shall have everything you need, my dear Joanna, and more.'

Together they walked down the wide track as people stared curiously at them and women murmured behind their hands. Kester favoured them all with an ironic bow, but Joanna kept her head up and her face to the front.

In the shelter of the forest he asked, 'Do you wish to tell me what they said?'

Memory made her flush and she shook her head.

'Well, it doesn't matter. I can guess that the woman with a mouth like a rat-trap found plenty to lash you with. I am truly sorry, Joanna. The delay was too much for the

men. They know what pleasures New Providence holds
for them. They will be punished,' he added grimly.

They resumed their walk and Joanna struggled to
comprehend her tangled emotions. A part of her was
bitter at the infamous way she had been treated and
apprehensive at the loss of her good name; another, and
larger part, was singing in abandoned joy that she was
once more beside the man she could not help loving.

Lovejoy caught them up in a rush, trailing some of
Joanna's possessions, and they were rowed back to the
Lady Margaret where Joanna settled into the main cabin
as if she had never left it, and when the truant men had
been rounded up and Jennison returned, the ship sailed
on the first tide.

Kester and Joanna ate an evening meal together,
tended by Lovejoy and Will Buckley who found it impossible to hide his delight at Joanna's return.

As they lingered over sweetmeats and wine, Kester
dismissed the servants and took her hand, 'Do you find
life aboard the *Lady Margaret* congenial to you?'

Congenial? It was a trivial word to describe the fulfilment he gave her, but she could never tell him so. He
might be a privateer, but she did not doubt he expected a
gentlewoman to act with proper decorum. She would
not risk embarrassing him and humiliating herself by
confessing a love unsought and unwanted.

So she replied rather primly that she enjoyed life at
sea.

He nodded, his eyes shadowed. 'That is what I
surmised. Have you considered your future after the
episode of New Providence?'

Her heart contracted. 'I have been trying to put it
from my mind, but I daresay I shall never again be
accepted by righteous people.'

His mouth twisted in derision. 'Among persons who
profess such smug self-satisfaction as your erst-while
betrothed and his friends, perhaps, though I do not

believe that all Puritans are so narrow in their views and so lacking in human kindness.'

She looked at him in quick surprise and a rueful smile touched his face. 'My vision of Puritans has been somewhat modified by contact with you, Joanna.' He continued: 'I am not a pirate, but a privateer and of gentle birth and therefore welcomed by quite exalted company.'

'I know the Modyfords to be your friends.'

'Not only them; I have good relations with many American people who live further north and plenty in Britain would be pleased to court my acquaintance.'

'Why are you telling me this? I believe you, but do not see how it can affect me.'

He looked at her thoughtfully, his dark eyes watchful. 'I am deeply concerned for your future. The news of your rejection by that . . . that mealy-mouthed man will soon whip round the islands. News travels here in a miraculous way. After that it cannot be long before it is known in Britain. I can think of one way only to protect you. You like me, do you not?'

She nodded, too choked to speak, and he said, 'Unions have been founded—have thrived—on far less. As Lady Venn your position would be secure.'

She went cold. He was offering her a loveless marriage to save her reputation. Loveless on his side, that was. The thought of belonging to him gave her a deep warmth, yet she was afraid, doubting her capacity to live with him as his wife, loving him as she did, knowing that anything he gave would be simply out of liking or, worse, compassion for her helplessness.

He frowned as she hesitated, then smiled in a way which made her weak. 'Marriage is a big step, Joanna, and not to be taken lightly, and normally you would have time to consider, but it is imperative that we arrive in Jamaica prepared to marry at once. You need say nothing to anyone, but I shall allow it to be understood that mistaken stories are emanating from New Providence.'

He rose and put a strong hand beneath her elbow, lifting her to her feet, and led her outside and up to the poop deck. They were concealed here by rigging and darkness was swiftly eating up the brilliance of the crimson sun on the deep blue horizon. A lazy breeze flapped the sails over their heads and the tang of salt mingled with the smell of vegetation wafted from one of the ever-near islands filling her nostrils and adding to the strange, aching yearning inside her. She leaned on the rail and stared into the sea, watching the wash of waves against the timbers. Kester turned her to face him and drew her near. His lips found hers in a kiss of exquisite tenderness.

'Do not refuse, Joanna. I swear to be good to you. I have never before considered the possibility of offering marriage to any woman. I never thought I would, but you . . .'

She held her breath. Was he about to tell her what she longed to hear? That he loved her.

'You are the most perfect woman I have ever met. You are pure in body, mind and spirit. I would be honoured to make you my wife. Please, say you will marry me.'

Her disappointment was superseded by euphoria which stole over her, modifying her judgment. What did it signify that he did not love her? She had enough for both of them and maybe in time . . . She was sure he would make a kind enough husband.

'I accept your offer, Kester. I will wed you.'

Joanna thought that Will Buckley showed the joy normally experienced by a bridegroom when he heard the news, acting as if he had personally engineered the whole matter, his narrow face a mask of satisfaction. He spent much of the time before they reached Jamaica going through his master's clothes, eventually pronouncing that nothing was fine enough to be wed in and insisting that fine brocades and silks be bought for the wedding attire.

Kester grinned. He was in an affable mood, pardoning the men who had slipped ashore, in honour of his betrothal, which made their toasts of congratulation all the more heartfelt.

There was a different mood aboard the vessel. Men who had regarded Joanna with speculative eyes or lascivious grins now treated her with respect. It seemed that buccaneers entertained a surprising reverence for marriage—if it concerned one of themselves.

The blue mountains of Jamaica rose from the sea to greet them and soon the *Lady Margaret* was anchored in the halfmoon harbour. Kester went ashore immediately and returned with an invitation from the King's House that Joanna should be a guest there and celebrate her marriage from its shelter.

She walked with Kester through Port Royal, watching with absorbed interest the teeming, bustling life. She had been so long away from civilisation, though much of what she saw could scarcely be dignified by such a title. Scores of men in all manner of motley garb swarmed the streets, staggering in and out of the dozens of alehouses, always adding to their intake of rum and wine. Women whose occupation there was no difficulty in recognising clung to their arms, ever-ready to grab at pieces of eight, Spanish doubloons, the louis d'or of France, the daalder of Holland, or any of the multitude of coins from all parts of the world, or any trinkets carried by the men. There were regular seamen from merchant ships and sailors of the King's Navy clad in their wide canvas breeches and blue jackets, many of them so ragged and sick looking that they brought forth her pity.

Kester's lip curled. 'Is it any wonder that we recruit some of our best men from them? They are so badly used by authority that they leap at an opportunity to get rich and our life is at least no harder than the one they leave.'

'Riches are not the ultimate aim of mankind,' said Joanna.

A shadow passed over Kester's face and she felt chilled. 'Always my little Puritan. But do not think all men become outlaws of the high seas only for money. Most of the poor souls in regular service seldom get enough to eat and their victuals are a disgrace.'

'You always have an excuse for lawlessness,' exclaimed Joanna, a sob escaping her.

They had reached the outskirts of the town and Kester stopped to look at her. His face was severe, his eyes cool, as he asked, 'Are you already regretting your decision to marry me?'

'I . . . I did not say so.'

'You are implying it in your criticisms! I will not have a wife for ever whining about our lives.'

Joanna's temper flared and words of bitter repudiation hovered on her lips. She stemmed them with an effort, staring into his dark eyes, suddenly overwhelmed by desire that he should woo her with soft words and loving caresses. She wanted him. No matter what he was she would love him forever.

She began to walk slowly towards the trees lining the road out of town and he followed. 'Well, Joanna?'

'I will—do my utmost—to conform with your life as you live it,' she promised. Her words were simple, but her mind was a mass of conflict as all the years of her righteous upbringing warred with her aching need for this man's love.

The beauty of the island seemed to underline her longing as they walked beneath trees of mahogany and cedar, ebony and rosewood, their browns and greens frequently enlivened by the brilliance of red, orange and yellow flowers which climbed from the forest floor to embrace the wide trunks and entwine the leaves.

The scents and sounds were drugging her and her amazement was profound when they reached a place where unbelievable toil had felled a large part of the jungle to give space to the domain of the Modyfords. Not for them the rudely built dwelling of brick floor, mountain timber walls and thatched roof, but a mansion surrounded by gardens filled with bright blossom and luscious vegetables and fruits all tended by a multitude of slaves.

Elizabeth Modyford, gentle eyed and welcoming, greeted them as a slave admitted them to the hall. She took Joanna's hands in hers and smiled. 'Kester! What a beautiful child! No wonder you have settled for marriage at last!'

She slipped her arm through Joanna's. 'Come, my dear, I will conduct you myself to your chamber. I wondered what kind of maid tempted the wayward Raven into the haven of matrimony.'

A man in blue coat slashed with silver emerged from a room and gave a loud laugh. 'Haven, indeed! Fortunate are they who can say as much.'

Lady Modyford presented the man as her husband, the Governor of Jamaica, who clearly regarded his pretty wife with deep affection, and the two women climbed the graceful stairway to an upper gallery. At the head of the stairs Joanna turned and saw that Kester was watching her. He touched his fingers to his forehead in a salute and disappeared into a room with Sir Thomas.

Joanna was led into a large bedchamber with blue and gold tapestry hangings and soft Chinese carpets of many-hued silks. Pink and blue brocade curtains hung at window and bed which was covered by a blue satin quilt, and a pink velvet chair and matching footstool stood near a small, carved table. The carving was repeated in two chests of drawers and several mirrors. Joanna revelled in the beauty of the room, expressing her delight, and assuring her pleased hostess that she could not fail to be comfortable and happy here. She gasped with

appreciation at the sight of a nosegay in a tiny jade vase
on a French escritoire and hurried to it, burying her face
in the fragrant blossoms. A damask rose, sweet williams,
a streaked gillyflower were bunched with marjoram and
rue and the mingled perfumes reminded her of her
garden in England and brought an aching lump to her
throat.

Lady Modyford touched her arm gently, 'I brought
the seeds with me when I joined Thomas. The rose I
reared from a tiny bush. I never thought to see them
survive, but here anything is possible. They remind me
of home.'

She left Joanna to the ministrations of three white-
clad slaves. She gave no intimation that she remembered
the night when she peered down a hatch on the *Lady
Margaret* and caught a glimpse of a woman aboard a
privateer's vessel, or of Joanna's repudiation by Master
Matthias Kemp, though undoubtedly she would by now
have heard, and Joanna was grateful for her forbearance.

The eldest slave announced herself as Hannah, laughing and showing strong white teeth in a dark face when
Joanna said she did not need so many handmaidens
and suggesting that they might be needed in the house-
work.

'Bless you, ma'am, we's upstairs maids. There's nigh
on a hundred indoor servants to do the work and it's a
nice change for us to have a different lady to wait on,
'specially a lovely young one like you.'

Lovejoy arrived, carrying Joanna's personal toiletries
which looked niggardly in the sumptuous room and she
informed the other women firmly that her new master
had purchased many far more grand things for his future
bride, and left them in no doubt that although she might
have been below them in status once she was now their
equal.

She and the two younger women went out and re-

turned bearing arms full of materials which spilled ove
the room in a riot of purple and crimson, green and gold
yellow and snowy white. Joanna smoothed the velvets
brocades, muslins and satins and fingered the filmy deli
cacy of the soft linens intended for her shifts and nigh
attire. Hot water was poured into a huge ewer and the
women stripped her and washed her from head to toe
then Hannah dipped her hands into lavender-scented oi
and massaged Joanna's silken skin. Her protests died
before the disregard of the slaves, who seemed to have
no aim in life but that of smoothing away any roughnes
induced by sun and sea-wind and rendering her even
more enticing for her wedding day.

As soon as Joanna wore a shift the door was opened to
a further collection of chattering slaves who came armed
with measuring tapes, pins and cotton, and who ex
claimed over her firm flesh as they called figures to the
head sewing slave who noted them down on a writing
tablet. Then Joanna must state her preference for cloth
and colour, giving precedence to her wedding gown. She
was so bemused by all the attention after her weeks at
sea that she had to ask advice of Lovejoy and the
head slaves who helped her to arrive at a satisfactory
decision.

The tobacco-brown gown had been inspected by Han
nah with a grimace and removed and now Joanna was
informed that Lady Modyford had insisted on lending
garments from her own wardrobe until the new ones
could be sewn. The senior slave produced a gown which
startled Joanna with its richness, but she had no choice
but to allow herself to be laced into a white bodice with
green stripes, the cords pulled hard to encompass a waist
more slender than the gown had been fashioned for
with a skirt of green brocade pinned up at the sides to
reveal a petticoat of stiff pink satin. A deep lace collar
matched several ruffles which fell from her elbows to
her wrists and knots of green ribbon completed the

ensemble. It was the most elaborate and colourful dress she had ever worn and as she surveyed herself in the mirror she wondered fleetingly what her father would have said, then she was seated and Hannah and Lovejoy busied themselves with hairbrush, unguents and curling irons until they considered her toilette completed by her lovely hair falling in ringlets to her shoulders, adorned only with simple pink ribbon bows.

Hannah turned to the chest of drawers confidently, 'Where's madam's jewellery?'

Lovejoy looked chagrined as she told an incredulous Hannah that there was none, making up a tale that it had all been lost in a storm at sea to explain her mistress's seeming lack of consequence. Joanna's lips twitched as she descended the stairs, recalling her single pearl chain, modest brooches and earrings.

A gorgeously dressed gentleman waiting in the hall looked up and she was startled when she recognised Kester. He had changed into a black velvet coat and breeches and a dark-red silk waistcoat. The short coat sleeve was turned back at the elbow and a cascade of lace and silk frills descended to be caught at the wrist from where it flowed over his strong brown hands. His muscular legs were encased in black stockings and his height increased by the heels on his leather, silver-buckled shoes.

His eyes flickered with amusement when he saw her and Elizabeth Modyford joined him and smiled. 'You are amused, Kester, and rightly so. Of course the gown is quite unsuitable for so dainty a creature as your Joanna, yet methinks nothing could fail to enhance such beauty. You are a fortunate man to have won her.'

Joanna walked between them into a large panelled room filled with people. Men and women were introduced to her in bewildering numbers and she was relieved when they were all seated round a vast oak dining table and the guests applied themselves to the serious

business of eating and drinking. The meal was as lavish
as the appointments of the mansion promised and course
succeeded course. Soup and fish, pork and fowl, pies and
tarts, pastries and fruits were all placed on the table and
attacked by the hungry diners while the talk ranged over
a variety of subjects, including the cultivation of land
both here and in the other islands.

She gathered that Sir Thomas's estates were large and
wealthy and his crops varied. He also spoke freely of the
profits to be made from buying and selling black gold
and she knew a thrill of horror when she realised he
meant human beings.

She glanced at the many slaves who waited at table,
some dressed as gaudily as children's dolls, but their
faces remained impassive, and after listening to accounts
of the labour problems on the sugar and tobacco plantations she presumed them to prefer a softer life indoors if
they must be enslaved. Yet she could not help wondering if any of the women had stood on the slave block and
suffered the agonies of humiliation and shame she had
known. The final course was carried to the table; it was a
masterpiece of confectionery—a *gâteau de fête* covered
with frosted rose leaves and violet petals with gilded
nuts, after which the guests lingered over wine and nuts
and most of the slaves withdrew. The talk turned to
matters of fighting, the women taking as much interest as
the men. The names of Puerto Bello, San Geronimo, La
Gloria and others entered the conversation and, for
Joanna, places which previously had figured only as
names on her father's atlas, became venues where men
and women had fought and died, plundered or been
made poverty-stricken, performed acts of cruelty or no-
bility. And through all the name of Henry Morgan
dominated.

Sir Thomas was the first to mention the fiery
Welshman, speaking of exploits performed beneath the
protection of his letter of marque. His grave counte-

nance expressed admiration as he said, 'He needs as many men and ships as he can get.'

'That is true,' exclaimed a Captain Collier. 'I intend to rejoin him tomorrow.'

'What are his plans?' asked Lady Modyford. 'You are his most trusted friend and must surely know.'

Edward Collier's eyes shone. 'Henry is keeping his own counsel at present. There is much speculation, but the town of Panama is the prize I think he has set his heart on. I think if once he conquers there he will retire from privateering and settle down.'

There was a roar of mirth at the idea of Morgan turning into a quiet householder. As it died away Collier said to Kester, 'What of you, sir? Henry spoke most particularly of you. He knows, as do we all, of your vow to prosecute attacks on Spaniards until we succeed in taking this part of the globe for Britain.'

Joanna held her breath, her eyes dilating. In her preoccupation with the approaching nuptials she had allowed Kester's violent calling to slide from her mind. Now she was forced to remember the restlessness of the buccaneers left aboard the *Lady Margaret* and the raucous quarrels which broke out more and more frequently.

Will had explained, 'They're bored, mistress. They've spent their share of the booty and want more. They always want more. Improvident as children, most of them.'

She prayed inwardly that Kester would refuse to join Henry Morgan on whatever bloody expedition he planned and her heart plumetted as he announced, 'As soon as Mistress Seldon and I are wed I shall be sailing for the *Isle des Vaches*. I have Henry's invitation.'

The conversation turned to the wealth of Panama, gorged as she was with gold, filled with treasure from the pearl fisheries, rich from luscious fruit plantations and teeming slave markets, dignified by great houses and grand churches which were crowned by the cathedral of Saint Anastasius.

One or two of the portly planters who had retired from privateering to run their rich estates became fired by the talk and declared that they would fit up a vessel and sail once more with Morgan, but a Captain John Morris sounded a warning.

'I cannot believe that Henry will try for Panama. Situated as it is on the other side of the isthmus it is well nigh inaccessible. Think of the swamps and jungle to be negotiated, and the Indian population who are murderous devils and who will spy or kill as readily for the Spaniards as for us. There can be no hope of surprise.'

Kester shrugged. 'Henry Morgan will not let such considerations deter him if he thinks he can succeed, and if anyone can it is he. His brilliant leadership could win the day. I am ready to trust him.'

There was a roar of acclaim in which the womenfolk, to Joanna's surprise, joined, and a toast was drunk to Henry Morgan and the damnation of his enemies and those of Britain.

A small lull followed and Joanna forced herself to say shakily, 'The British Government is anxious surely to maintain good relations with Spain at the moment. Such a raid must damage their intent.'

The entire company turned and stared at her, but she saw only Kester's frown as he said, 'Spain has already broken her treaty and must pay the consequence.'

Joanna subsided and remained silent. She saw the gentle eyes of Elizabeth Modyford on her and was puzzled as to how such a moderate person could view with such seeming equanimity the warlike propensities of her guests.

She retired that night with her head buzzing. After the maids had helped her to prepare for bed and settled her down she lay thinking and was assailed again by the thrill of terror which had shaken her at the name of Panama.

Try as she might she could not rid herself of the convic-
tion somehow the town was destined to take on meaning
which would prove horrible for herself and Kester.

CHAPTER
NINE

THE day of the wedding dawned sunny and warm with a scattering of tiny white clouds in the blue bowl of the sky. Kester was not staying in the King's House and Joanna had learned that he owned a moderate estate in the foothills to which she would accompany him after the wedding. Her gowns had been cut and fitted by the sewing slaves who had been directed to work only for the bride.

The night before her wedding Lady Modyford had come to Joanna as she lay in the fourposter and stood for a moment looking down at her before saying, 'A word of advice, my dear. You protested at the idea of attacking Spanish possessions the first night you were here. Do not undermine Kester with soft women's talk. We all share your terror of the terrible fighting and the idea of losing the men we love, but we hold our peace. A man must go wholeheartedly to battle or his lack of concentration may cost him his life, or at best, serious injury.'

Joanna found it impossible to reply and Lady Modyford looked compassionately into the wide blue eyes and pressed her hand. 'Perhaps Kester will decide to leave his precarious existence when you begin to bear your children. You must hope, my dear.'

She left, snuffing out the lamp, and Joanna lay in the dark, still missing the slip-slap of waves on the hull of the *Lady Margaret*, unable to find rest. The mention of children had brought her marriage into sharp focus. Soon she would belong completely to Kester Venn. She turned her face to the orris-scented pillows, wondering how she would endure the knowledge that although she would be giving herself in love he would not know it, nor wish to do so, and would be giving her only what other women had known in casual profligacy.

Before the slaves began to dress her for her nuptials and while she was still alone Joanna examined herself in the long mirror and knew that she was beautiful for her bridegroom. At home her only looking glass had been a small hand-held one and even that was frowned upon in the strict Puritan household. Never before had she beheld herself entirely unclothed. She wondered if Kester would find her body pleasing and was shocked at her wild hope that she would fire him with desire.

Then she slipped beneath the bed covers as she heard the approach of the chattering, giggling slaves and the ritual of dressing began. First she was bathed and perfumed before being buttoned into a snowy shift. Petticoats were draped around her and tied at the waist; two of white lawn and one of blue lutestring. Knitted stockings of pink silk were drawn over her slender legs and secured with blue garters and she slid her feet into blue satin shoes with high heels and her hands into long white gloves of scented kid. Then Lovejoy and Hannah eased her into her wedding gown of palest blue damask with an overskirt of azure taffeta drawn back with azure velvet bows and ending in a tiny train. The long pointed waistline and low bodice embroidered with flower patterns of seed pearls displayed as much of her feminine charms as it concealed. Joanna was no longer shocked. She knew an instant's panic as she realised that she was swiftly forgetting the principles instilled in her with severe, but loving care by her parents, and felt a yearning for her father's approval and for the loving ministrations of the familiar maids who had died at sea.

Lovejoy chided her gently on her melancholy face. 'There's women all over the islands would give their souls to step into your shoes,' she grinned.

Joanna was given no time to assimilate this statement as she was ordered by Hannah to stand up straight while

the maids climbed on stools to put the finishing touches
to hair already brushed and curled. They drew back the
shining tresses into a large knot, leaving tendrils of gold
to tumble about her ears and forehead. Then they placed
a small, round cap of transparent lace over her crown
and secured it with small silver pins and a pale pink bow.
Joanna surveyed herself, scarcely believing that this
elegant creature could be Joanna Seldon.

Lovejoy was frowning and muttering crossly about
her mistress's lack of jewels when a slave entered bearing a box, followed by Lady Modyford. 'Your bridegroom has sent his wedding gifts,' she announced.

There were gasps as Joanna opened the box lined in
purple velvet and lifted out a necklace of exquisitely fine
gold set with perfect sapphires, and a pair of eardrops to
match. Even a Puritan maid was not denied pierced ears
and Lady Modyford threaded the fine gold wire through
Joanna's lobes and fastened the necklace around her
long throat.

'It is exactly right,' she said with satisfaction. 'Kester
asked me the hue of your gown and chose the jewels to
match.'

Colour ran up under Joanna's skin. 'Are they . . . did
he . . . buy them?'

Elizabeth Modyford's white brow creased. 'You are
wondering if they are privateer's booty, I do not know.
However he acquired them he did it fairly, of that you
may be sure. Why, my own favourite gems came from a
marauding Spanish ship.'

Courtesy toward her hostess forbade another word
and Lady Modyford, finding Joanna pliant, smiled, and
put her arms about her and kissed her cheek. 'There, my
dear, in lieu of a mother's kiss. I wish you may have as
much happiness as I do with my dear Thomas.'

A carriage, polished and decorated with garlands, was
waiting at the door, the matched grey horses tossing
heads adorned with flowers and ribbons and Sir Thomas,

who was standing for Joanna's father, handed her in. The drive through forest and plantation to the white stone church was conducted in silence, Joanna feeling as if she were in a dream. She had always visualised her marriage as a simple affair in the privacy of her home, surrounded by soberly clad, grave fellow Puritans; or in a quiet parlour or meeting house on New Providence.

Instead she was led into the ornamented and flower filled church to the strains of music and the high, sweet voices of choirboys. A little girl carrying a silver gilt bride cup filled with gilded rosemary and bay led the way, her tiny form held erect in spite of the weight of her grand brocade dress, and Joanna walked between a concourse of men and women whose clothing vied with the island birds of paradise in their splendid colours, and whose gems caught sparks from the slanting sun and filled the church with thousands of dancing lights, while the plumes of their hats nodded like a field of brilliant corn.

Kester waited for her at the altar in burgundy brocade and black velvet, but even his smile did not bring reality closer and she listened unbelieving to the sound of her own voice giving the responses. When the priest droned a name—Christopher Venn—it took a moment for her to realise that she was hearing Kester's baptisimal name. Then they were exchanging rings, the music swelled and bells pealed and she and Kester were walking down the aisle and out into the sunshine to receive congratulations from the large congregation which followed them back to the King's House where there was to be a celebration.

Joanna stood with Kester at the end of the long reception room in a bower of tropical flowers, scarlet and emerald green, gold and crimson, and felt that her transition from Puritan maid to wife of a Royalist privateer was epitomised in the contrast between a modest English nosegay and this burst of colour.

She picked at the rich food, managing only a little cold chicken and whipped syllabub and Kester also appeared not to be hungry, though he took freely of wine at the many toasts. The wedding favours, true-love knots of blue and silver ribbons were distributed, and at the conclusion of the meal a platter bearing a wonderful confection of iced sugar was set before Joanna and Kester who leaned over to exchange a kiss amid much laughter and advice, both humorous and frank. Then the platter was lifted high and the icing broken to release a shower of tiny bride-cakes on the heads of the couple and their guests.

A small band of musicians struck up and Kester and Joanna led the dancing with a slow *courante*, performing the dance *à deux* with fluent ease on Kester's part and, on Joanna's, a concentrated determination to remember Lady Modyford's lessons. When the dancing was at its height and the company anticipated the Masque Kester touched Joanna's arm with a proprietorial air and announced that it was expedient to slip away.

'I have arranged for us to go straight to my home in the foothills,' he explained, an ironic smile on his lips, 'where we shall not be subjected to displays of lewd horseplay. No one can get past my guard-slaves and dogs.'

And with carefully planned efficiency Joanna found herself taking grateful leave of Sir Thomas and Lady Elizabeth Modyford and being lifted on to the side saddle of a graceful brown mare. Kester mounted an ebony stallion and, taking the mare's bridle, led his wife through the gates of the King's House and on to the forest track leading to the hills.

The sun was sinking, reflecting blood red on the clouds as they emerged from the forest into the clearing which contained Kester's house. It was elegant, white with slim pillars supporting a porch, the latticed windows flanked by olive green shutters. Gardens surrounded it and the air was redolent with the scents of flowers and foliage still hot from the sun.

The slaves were leaving their work and passed them carrying hoes and shovels over their shoulders. They bent their knee as their master and his bride went by and Joanna thought that their words of congratulation sounded sincere. She had observed that her new husband was a strict but good master on board ship and she supposed he was as just on land.

Lovejoy had gone ahead and waited for them beside a white-haired butler and plump housekeeper who welcomed them with broad smiles as Kester handed his bride up the wide, shallow steps to the large, studded front door.

The hall was cooled by fans swung to and fro on cords attached to the wrists of small slave boys in white and Joanna noted with approval that Kester's house servants wore simple white and not one was garbed in the gaudy doll-like outfits she had hated. Some of the women topped their gowns with a bright scarf and all appeared well fed and happy.

She walked with her husband into a drawing room furnished in ebony and mahogany, much of which was carved and inlaid. The drapes were of crimson and gold, matching an upholstered couch on which Joanna sat to drink the juice of oranges, lemons and limes sweetened with sugar grown and processed on the island.

Just before the sun set she and Kester walked in the kitchen gardens, and he pointed out breadfruit and yams, peas and sweet potatoes, and the deadly cassava root which the Indians had learned to tame for their own use. He bent sometimes to lift a leaf, or talk knowledgably to a garden slave who lingered among the plants, and Joanna realised that if life had not wrested all that he held dear from him he would have settled contentedly as a farmer.

Then the sun was gone and they returned to the house.

They were lighted up the stairs and into a bedchamber where the furniture was all rosewood, elegantly carved, explained Kester, by an artistic slave, then he left her to complete her toilette in privacy. Lovejoy assisted her out of her formal clothes and bathed her in scented water, bringing her one of the new bedgowns of lawn and lace. She laid aside the little lace cap and brushed her mistress's hair until it hung over her shoulders like a gold silk mantle, and Joanna climbed into the fourposter bed and lay between sheets of heavy linen which surely must have come from England. As she leaned back against the soft pillows Lovejoy smoothed the folds of the bed curtains of white silk with tiny embroidered yellow and lavender flowers entwined with green stems and patted the matching counterpane, before smiling encouragingly and disappearing through the door, closing it gently behind her.

Joanna waited, wondering if Kester meant to come to her tonight, or at all, or if he had decided to accept the marriage as one of convenience and continue to take mistresses to ease his body. She scarcely knew what she hoped for, at one moment willing him to find her irresistible, at the next outraged at the idea of being possessed by a man who did not love her.

She did not at first realise that a door which was hidden behind a wall hanging between two carved chests had opened to admit her husband. Kester was with her almost soundlessly, his tall form wrapped in a richly embroidered dressing gown reaching to his ankles. It made him appear taller than ever and the ruby-red silk gave his face a darker, more saturnine appearance.

He recognised her quick apprehension and smiled and said softly, 'You must not fear me, Joanna. I promise to be gentle.'

Then the mantle was thrown over a chair and he slid into bed beside her, his body naked as when she had seen him swimming. She froze, waiting his next move, her mind tumbling over the strictures of her old nurse as she had briefly described the duties of a gentlewoman in the marriage bed. He touched her with infinite care, stroking her hair and face, his lips seeking hers and roving over her with forbearance until her body responded and her nervousness fled on the wings of desire and she slid her arms about him, drawing him to her. At once his tentative approach gave way to urgency as he sensed her need and his muscles tautened. They fused in a fire of mutual passion and Joanna forgot everything as she was lifted to heights of sensation of which she could never have dreamed.

Afterwards they lay close, his arm around her, his hand caressing her silken skin, and she glanced into his face to find him looking at her with an ardent tenderness which left her breathless. Would he utter now the words of love she longed to hear? But as he sensed her watchfulness the look vanished and he pulled his arm from beneath her and drew the covers over them both. He turned from her and blew out the lamp and within minutes his deep breathing told her he was asleep, but she was wakeful, veering from a tranquil fulfilment to an impulse to shake her husband awake and demand . . . what? He could not force himself to love her in truth. She had only to think of Matthias to know that love could not be manufactured. The mere thought of her former betrothed made her realise that the notion of sharing with him in the marriage bed the intimacy she had discovered with Kester would have darkened her life.

Her horror that she would have been legally and morally bound to accept his lovemaking whenever he so desired made her marvel that a man could apparently enter a woman's body simply as an act of physical need. She had been taught that this was so; warned not to demand more of a husband than he could give, but she had never understood what such a situation could mean to a woman in love. Now she did and she burned at the admission that she had betrayed her ardour to a man who did not love her. Next time she would hold back. But when her restlessness disturbed Kester and he reached out for her and drew her close all her resolution fled in the face of his skill and again every nerve in her yielding flesh reacted as if he were a master musician and she an instrument from which he drew exquisite rhythms.

Their ecstasy soared to even greater heights as Joanna forgot everything but a primitive urge to give and receive love.

When she awoke from a deep sleep the sun was drawing steam from the earth and when Lovejoy opened a casement the garden scents filled her nostrils.

'This is surely a lovely place,' she enthused to her mistress. 'Will you rise or eat in bed? There's eggs and slices of pork, new baked bread and honey. I've eaten till I could pop.'

Joanna could not rest and rose and gowned herself in a rose taminy petticoat with a flowered overskirt and followed Lovejoy to a small parlour flooded by sunlight and overlooking the flower garden, where she breakfasted on bread and honey and milk.

She longed to know where Kester was, but would not ask, and when his tall form blotted out the light as he stepped over the low windowsill she became tongue-tied with shyness. He bent over her in a formal bow and kissed her hand, laughing at her. His fine linen shirt was open almost to the waist, his breeches were of rough homespun and his shoes plain brown leather and she had a fleeting memory of him as she had first seen him. The Raven, black-garbed to match his soul, she had believed. But perhaps her first impression was right. What had changed, apart from her own circumstances? But she loved him and somehow she must win his love— she must!

He pulled her to her feet and patted her rear with husbandly familiarity. 'Go get your woman to find you some strong boots so we can go walking.'

Soon they were striding through the gardens until they reached fern and moss covered rocks at the end and Kester showed her the easiest way to climb them, patiently fitting her feet into holds, helping her to control her long skirts.

'If you are to accompany me you had best wear breeches, I think.'

'Like Claris, I suppose.'

The name fell between them like a challenge and split the blue and gold day like a knife in a peach. Joanna bit her lip and straightened. They had climbed high enough to see the sea stretching into the distance, broken here and there by the inevitable cays, meeting the sky in a haze impossible to define. Kester moved on and she followed him to a track where the going was easier. It led among trees through which she heard the rush of water and they arrived at the side of the pool which was kept clear by a high waterfall tumbling and sparkling in the sun filtering through the leaves. The deep pool spilled over forming another fall and the river disappeared among the greenery on its way to the sea.

There was a patch of short turf on the bank and Kester knelt and held out his arms, his eyes giving her an invitation which sent blood coursing through her veins. Wordlessly she sank with him to the grass and their bodies united to renew their passion to the rippling music of the water.

She lay back and watched Kester as he stood on the river's edge, his skin sun-dappled, then he dived with scarcely a splash. He swam across the pool, returned and climbed out in a lithe movement and stood before her, water streaming over his skin from his black hair.

'Join me,' he said, 'the water is wonderful.'

She stared, a small smile touching her lips. 'You jest!

Who ever heard of a gentlewoman bathing out of doors?'

'As the bride of a privateer you had best learn to swim,' he grinned. 'Come, woman, do I have to remove the rest of your clothes myself? Not that I object, you understand . . .'

She flushed at his intimate smile, but her inhibitions died as they always did when this man commanded and he assisted her to undo tapes and buttons until she stood by him, her hair hanging loose, only a cotton shift hiding her nakedness.

Kester took her to a part where rocks descended in natural steps and she lowered herself into the water, gasping at the coolness after the heat of the sun. With his strong hands to support her she took her first lesson in swimming, finding the sensation of floating with only one of his hands to keep her afloat a sensation of un-imagined bliss.

They dried themselves in the sun and returned to the house, laughing like children at play, completely con-genial, to devour enormous quantities of the good food awaiting them.

A week went by, the days strung together like lustrous jewels on a golden chain, as they walked, climbed and rode together, swam in the secluded pool and made love with increasingly abandoned pleasure, ate, talked, jested and slept and Joanna tasted happiness which was almost perfect.

She could not tell when the prickle of uneasiness began. Perhaps it had been there from the first, a gnaw-ing certainty that Kester was waiting only for the right moment to confront her with some unpleasant reality.

On the eighth day after the wedding he was lying by her side at the pool. They had made love until they were satiated, then she had swum across the pool alone. She was still tingling with a sense of achievement at his praise, but as she caught his watchful expression she was afraid and tried to distract him by running her finger over the dark hairs on his chest, smiling teasingly at him.

He held her wrist, refusing to be cajoled. 'This existence will not do, Joanna.'

Still she tried to pretend, pouting at him like a coquette and saying, 'I thought I was making you happy.'

A shadow passed over his face. 'Happy? Aye, you have made me exceedingly content.'

'But it is all an illusion?' Her tone was disappointed.

'I have wronged you.'

'That is past. You are kind to me now and I . . .'

'You should have been permitted to follow your destiny. You should have been the wife of your respectable Matthias.'

Her heart lurched. 'You are tired of me!'

He gave an exasperated snort. 'How like a woman! I make a true observation and you jump to a false conclusion.'

He ran his hand over the slope of her shoulder and her gently curving bosom. 'A man could never grow weary of such loveliness, Joanna. Certainly not I!'

She sat up abruptly, disturbing a vermilion fly-catcher bird which had swooped in to grasp its prey. She wanted him to care for more than just her body, but it seemed he did not. It was a lesson she was constantly having to relearn.

'How long will you be pleased to live this half-life?' he asked. 'You are cut off from all you held dear.' He stopped, then continued slowly, 'You have a right to see your father, if only to reassure him of your wellbeing.'

Dismay flooded her and she was not quick enough to hide it. He gripped her arm painfully, jerking himself up so that he could see her face fully. 'You do not wish to see him?'

'Of course I do, Kester. I love him!'

'I do not doubt it and I recognise your right—your

need—to see your family. I am offering to take you to England.'

'To leave me there?' Surely he could not miss the bleakness in her.

'No! You are my wife! You must follow where I go.'

She saw that he misinterpreted her meaning. He thought she would prefer to stay in England without him. She said, 'I accept my . . . my duty as your wife, Kester. I am . . . content to do so. Surely it would be best to allow matters to remain as they are. If we go to England . . .'

He stared at her, anger clouding his dark eyes. 'By God, I believe you do not want me to meet your father!'

Goaded she burst out, 'Is that so strange? Can you imagine arriving in the quiet little town where I was born and announcing to everyone that its leading Puritan citizen's daughter is wed to a royalist, and worse, to a privateer? A man who has amassed his fortune by looting and fighting.'

He hung on to his temper with an effort. 'Allow me some discretion. I will travel as a private gentleman and explain exactly what happened in the past. If your father is a good Christian surely he will understand and forgive.'

'Maybe he would—maybe not!' She tried to visualise her father's scholarly face, to gauge his reaction to such a revelation. She drew to mind the faces of the Puritan gentlemen who made up his circle of friends. There were those who would denounce Kester for a villain and spurn any who harboured him. Her father had suffered considerably in the troubled years of religious differences which he believed had shortened her mother's life. How could she bring him further anguish? And if her father and husband quarrelled how would she endure it?

Kester sprang to his feet. 'By God, you are ashamed of me! I believed you a woman of courage!'

She too rose and stared up at him. 'I am not ashamed of anything *I* have done.'

'Of course, madam, the wrong is all on my side, is that it? I am the one who defiled and corrupted innocence.'

'If you say so!' she flashed, her temper rising to meet his.

She wished she had controlled her unruly tongue. She longed to explain that the idea of enmity between the two people she loved above all others was too great a risk for her to contemplate. Perhaps in time . . . if only he would grant her time to get used to the idea.

His own hurt exploded in words. 'I suppose it never occurred to you that if *my* family were still on earth they would be equally horrified to find me wed to a ranting, canting Puritan!'

Joanna gasped. 'I am astonished that you could bring yourself to marry me. Oh, but of course, you sacrificed yourself in the cause of conscience—*yours*, may I remind you, and having done so you have fulfilled your *obligations* most admirably, bedding me with commendable thoroughness.'

His answer was caustic. 'To which you responded in a most un-Puritan-like way!'

Outrage, horror at the way their happiness had degenerated into an ugly quarrel held her fast for a second, then she raised her hand and struck his face with a crack which echoed through the dell.

Her fury was directed as much at herself as at him, but he could not be expected to know that and his rage matched hers. Her grabbed her shoulders and shook her. Then he held her still and his eyes darkened as he pulled her towards him.

She read his intention and struggled helplessly, 'No, I beg you . . . not in anger . . . please, Kester . . .'

Her protests were swamped beneath the onslaught of a desire more powerful because of their heightened emotions and the world became a fusion of painful frenzy.

He rolled away from her and lay still, staring into the
canopy of the sky, before he rose and pulled on his
clothes. She too scrambled up and dressed, her fingers
fumbling over tapes and pins. She looked once at him
and was shocked by the disgust written plainly on his
face.

As she stumbled down the mountain after him she was
consumed with regrets. Why had she not guarded her
tongue? Better to have lied than placed this barrier
between them. She loved him so and now she had destroyed their tenuous relationship. He had insulted her
faith, but only under provocation which had probably
been increased to immense proportions by his vulnera-
bility where his dead family was concerned. Any insult
to his way of life he no doubt saw as one offered his loved
ones.

At dinner, which they picked at in an air of an-
tagonism, he said, 'Two days ago an invitation reached
me to join Henry Morgan. He is amassing a fleet to make
a decisive stroke against the Spaniards. I shall return to
my ship tonight and tomorrow I shall send Will to fetch
you.'

Her heart felt cold. Kester had resumed the cloak of
the Raven, unbending, severe, filled with mistrust and
dislike, but nothing altered her love and the thought of
his going into danger filled her with dread. If only she
had the right to plead with him not to go.

The bed seemed coldly empty that night and she slept
badly, aching for the comfort of his body beside her. On
the following day she was glad to leave the plantation
and she climbed aboard the *Lady Margaret* with Lovejoy, resolved to find a way through the barrier once they
shared the large fourposter bed.

Kester was engaged in the day cabin with several other
captains who were planning to sail with him and Joanna
closed the door of the inner cabin and stowed away her
new gowns, deeply conscious of the difference between

now and the first time she had been brought on board. She thought regretfully of their quarrel, and of what might have been, but surely Kester would not hold his anger hot. When they were alone, however, he treated her with cool courtesy and seemed entirely preoccupied by his plans. Tonight, she promised herself, I will make him want me and somehow I will restore our concord.

The moon was high when Kester joined her in the small cabin. Will had dragged off his boots and she heard him undress, lying still and wakeful. He blew out the swinging lamp and climbed in beside her. She waited, but he made no move and when she would have reached out to caress him she realised by his slow, even breathing that he was asleep.

Her sense of rejection filled her with deep mortification. She was now well aware of his passionate nature and writhed to realise how he must have held on to his self control to avoid making love to her.

He must have slaked his thirst with another woman! The idea sprang into her mind, and she thought of the many women from whom the Raven could take his pick.

She wished with all her heart that she had chosen her words more carefully. Now the fragile relationship they had been constructing was shattered and the fragments of its brittle shell pierced her heart like ice splinters.

Tears of misery and humiliation coursed down her cheeks. She longed for his embrace, but she would not let him know. Why lay herself open to further insult? He should make the advances. But she could not stop the tears and finally fell asleep on a damp pillow.

CHAPTER
TEN

THEY sailed early the next morning and at breakfast Kester continued to treat her as if she were a passenger, offering her distant politeness.

Goaded beyond endurance she burst out, 'If you intend behaving so coldly, you had best find another bed. It can scarce be considered seemly for such a stranger to occupy mine.'

His dark eyes regarded her with such coldness that she shivered. 'It seems I must remind you that we occupy *my* sleeping quarters. I have no intention of quitting them and raising lewd speculation on the part of the crew.'

'Surely, the *Raven* knows how to deal with impertinence!'

His glance raked her. 'Oh, my men do not doubt my prowess in the field of love, madam. Rather, it could be your failings which they would find amusing.'

Her face flamed. 'You know . . .' she gasped. 'You know I am . . .' She was unable to continue, her voice choked with indignation.

The sardonic smile which played around his shapely mouth and flickered in his eyes brought her to a panting fury which she bit back. Whatever she said he would see it as a chance to wound her.

When they anchored Joanna recognised the barren *Isle des Vaches*, but she was astonished at the forest of masts swaying in the swell of the waves. Will and Robert Jennison joined her on the rail. The surgeon regarded the busy scene with red-rimmed cynical eyes.

'They are massing for another raid,' he muttered. 'Well, we medical men will have the most to do, I reckon. That's how it usually turns out.'

Joanna shivered and Will chided him, 'Don't alarm
Lady Venn. She don't want to hear about your gory
work.'

Joanna could not get used to her new title which
seemed to underline the incongruity of her position. She
was wed to an English aristocrat, yet was on board a ship
about to join a company of men intent on a pillaging raid.

Kester came to her and the others slipped away.
Joanna asked, 'Where have all these vessels come from?
Who captains them?'

'Some, like myself, are Morgan's friends and col-
leagues. Others are naval men sent by Modyford. There
are French ships here too. We are all as one in our
determination to give a sharp lesson to our enemies.'

In the cabin Will laid out a fine outfit of black velvet
and white lace and Kester made ready to join his
fellows for dinner. He was rowed to Morgan's flag ship,
Satisfaction, leaving Joanna to sit discontentedly in the
cabin, watching lights beginning to flicker in the ships
and hearing burst of male laughter from the dinner
party.

She wandered on deck and looked up at the myriad
stars in the black sky, feeling her misery increase beneath the beautiful spell of the Caribbean night. Her
whole being cried out for her husband's arms about her,
his lips on hers, the movement of his hard body against
her tender flesh. Over on the *Satisfaction* his fate was
being discussed and decided and she, a mere woman,
had no part in such masculine matters, though his wellbeing was paramount in her concern.

She was on the point of retiring when the party broke
up with many loud good wishes and much mirth and the
captains were rowed to their own vessels. Kester
climbed over the ship's rail, the affability in his face
dying as he saw Joanna.

She followed him into the cabin. 'What was decided?'
she asked quietly, though her heart was hammering.

He stared at her for a moment and she thought he would refuse to reply, then he shrugged. 'We are going on an expedition which will be the most hazardous of Morgan's career—and of mine!'

She watched him seat himself apparently unconcernedly and pull his charts to him. She longed to plead with him not to run into danger. Elizabeth Modyford's warning came to her and reminded her she must not try to weaken her man with worries of danger, yet she loved him so . . .

He glanced up at her. 'Go to bed. I have plans to prepare.'

When she did not move he raised his brows. 'You wish to say something?'

'This expedition, Kester. You are looking forward to it, are you not?'

'I follow my trade of privateer. Can it be that you are concerned for my welfare?' He gave her no time to answer. 'Well, it will be dangerous, but we shall eventually muster around thirty-five ships and nigh on two thousand men. Enough to give the Spaniards a good roasting.'

'Where do you intend to go?'

'Have done with questions! Even Morgan is not yet decided on that.'

Her voice was almost a whisper as she asked, 'Will you—take me?'

He gave a short laugh. 'Women are forbidden to accompany us, a decision with which I agree. I have my own idea of what lies ahead and it will require all the strength of a man.'

He turned back to his charts in a dismissive gesture and Joanna walked into the inner cabin and prepared for bed. She lay wakeful until he joined her and did not close her eyes until long after he slept.

The next morning she awoke early after a restless night and rolled over to look at her still sleeping

husband. His face seemed younger in repose, all harshness smoothed away. She stared at his mobile mouth,
her own working in her intense desire to kiss it. If she
thought she had a hope of arousing him to desire she
would not hesitate to use all the wiles which her love had
taught her, but she was too afraid to risk the chance that
he might spurn her.

She slid out of bed and pulled on a lilac taffeta wrap-
per and walked out on deck. The sun was rising, touching the small clouds with rosy fingers and the air smelled
sweet. Sailors lay all over the decks, curled up like dogs
in any corner they could find, all sleeping. Only the man
on watch touched his turban to her before returning to
his post.

She had a sudden sensation that other eyes watched
her and turned quickly to see that a sloop had anchored
near them in the night. A figure sat huddled on a pile of
rope, staring fixedly at the *Lady Margaret* and Joanna's
heart almost stopped. It was Claris, wearing her garb of
breeches and shirt, but her long red hair was uncovered
and flowed down her back as if seeking to deny the
implication of masculine dress. It looked like a flag of
challenge and Joanna remembered what this woman had
been to her husband—and could be again.

Water slapped the hulls and a seabird called harshly
while the two women measured one another with cold
stares. Claris looked her hatred and when she was joined
by a leering Captain Pryce Joanna was filled with sick
revulsion. She felt rooted to the deck as they put their
heads together and whispered and Claris gave a
malignant laugh which broke the spell binding Joanna
who fled back to the cabin.

Her quick run awoke Kester who sat up, alert. 'Is
something amiss?'

'Your mistress is here,' she burst out.

The Raven yawned and stretched. 'Are you
surprised?'

'Evidently you are not. Perhaps you arranged an assignation.'

His sleepiness vanished. 'Do not be a fool! Claris would not turn aside from a chance of fighting Spaniards.'

'She is with Captain Pryce!'

She had the doubtful satisfaction of seeing his urbanity ruffled. 'Now I *am* surprised! She has no respect or liking for him.'

There was much consultation before it was decided that the assembled ships would sail to the isthmus and attack Panama. The orders were given and all the ships sprang to bustling life. Joanna was learning shipboard drill fast, but still the teeming complexity needed to take a sailing vessel to sea bewildered and fascinated her. The small anchorage rang to the orders of bo'suns and seamen in a variety of dress hauled on ropes, or clambered in rigging using hands and feet with almost equal aptitude as they hung at dizzy heights.

The fleet sailed before a favourable breeze, commanded by Henry Morgan who had been officially appointed Admiral and Commander in Chief with Edward Collier as his vice-admiral and the flags which streamed above the sails were all patriotic.

Their first port of call was the island of Santa Catarina. The governor had no stomach for taking on the massed buccaneers and relinquished the island and its forts in return for mercy towards the people. The seamen were then at liberty to swarm over the island, catching and slaughtering cattle and fowl while the veteran privateer, Captain Bradley, continued on to the River Chagres, the approach to Panama, the mouth of which was barred by the fortress of San Lorenzo. Although in the fierce fighting Bradley and thirty of his men died the fortress was taken and the remainder of the fleet sailed.

Arriving at the fortress all the captains went to inspect the severe damage and make final plans. Joanna was ordered to stay on board and watched her husband disappear up the steep hill towards the fortress walls feeling near despair. He acted towards her like a stranger as if the exigencies of war had completed his estrangement.

The half-savage crew who had waited so long for a chance to fight were restless and scuffles broke out repeatedly. No one but the Raven seemed able to keep them in order, but Joanna had grown so used to the incipient violence surrounding her that she did not bother even to look round when there was a cacophony of yells and whistles and she was taken by surprise when Claris appeared before her.

'How dare you return to this ship!' she exclaimed.

Claris shrugged. 'The Raven is ashore and it's you I want to see.'

'We have nothing to say to one another. After your filthy behaviour to me . . .'

'I was fighting for my man,' snarled Claris, her eyes flashing spite.

'He is not yours any longer!'

'No! I was afraid as soon as I saw you that he would want you even though you're a mealy-mouthed Puritan. But you'll not hold him. He doesn't love you.'

Joanna's stomach contracted in horror. Surely Kester had not discussed her with his former mistress. Her tongue clove to the roof of her mouth and Claris gave a twisted grin. 'He *couldn't* love you—not the Raven—not the man who lived with me and fought by my side. When he tires of you he'll send you away and I shall return.'

Joanna found her voice, 'You have not recently visited Jamaica?'

'What's that got to do with anything?'

'If you had you must have heard of our marriage . . .'

She stopped as shock robbed Claris's face of colour and sent her breath through her teeth in a hiss. 'Liar! He wouldn't . . .! He loves me . . . he was forced to sentence me in front of the men, but he bought leniency for me because he knew I would come back to him. He'll get tired of you. He'd *never* marry you!'

Will stepped between the women. 'It's true,' he said quietly. 'You'd best get back to Pryce. Funny sort of man for you to take up with!'

Claris thrust Will aside, her fury giving her added strength. She pushed her face close to Joanna's as she mouthed, 'I don't know how you tricked him into wedding you, Puritan, but I'll be revenged on you, see if I'm not!'

Then she ran for the side, swinging her legs over and half climbing, half sliding to the boat below to be rowed back to Pryce's vessel.

Joanna stared after her, sick at heart, then turned away. She had no doubt that Claris was capable of murdering her if only she could contrive it without being detected by Kester. And only Joanna and her husband knew that much of Claris's anger would turn to contemptuous amusement if she knew how swiftly Kester had discarded his wife.

When Kester learned later of Claris's visit he frowned heavily as Will finished, 'But Lady Venn won't be in danger while we're away from her because Claris will be sure to come to Panama.'

Kester shook his head. 'Captain Morgan has issued orders excluding women from this foray. The terrain will be the most difficult ever attempted.'

Will shook his head. 'I daresay Claris will disobey Captain Morgan.'

'If she does she will suffer the penalty handed to dissidents in war time, but I am more concerned with the safety of my wife.'

Claris gave no trouble when she learned of the ban and this increased Joanna's foreboding. She was relieved to be told that Kester had arranged for her to remain in the conquered fortress of San Lorenzo under the protection of Major Richard Norman, the newly appointed commander. Kester took her to the fortress and she was made welcome by Major Norman and shown to a chamber which had been repaired after the fierce battle. 'There is a small adjoining chamber for your maid,' said the major, 'and we shall endeavour to find you every comfort a place like this can afford.'

He left and Lovejoy went to the kitchens while Joanna looked from the narrow window down to where prisoners and buccaneers toiled to make the fortress habitable and render the earthworks protective. Fires had all but destroyed them and the men looked like industrious ants as they scurried about.

Kester was watching her. 'We move tomorrow. Tonight I shall stay with you.'

She searched his features for one sign of love, listened to his voice trying to detect a hint of affection. He expressed polite indifference. Lovejoy was sent to sleep somewhere else and Major Norman sent them as good a meal as he could manage and left them in peace. The small apartment had been quickly made more homely by the addition of a couple of wall hangings and an upholstered chair probably brought from the major's quarters and Joanna walked around restlessly, wondering what she could do to make the time pass while she was alone.

Her husband opened a sack and brought out two packages. The first contained some small rolls of linen and silk material and a quantity of skeins of silk of many shades. There were also needles, a thimble and scissors.

'I was afraid time would drag for you,' he said evenly. 'I hope these will make your wait more endurable.'

She took the skeins and slid them through her fingers. 'What a kind thought.' She secretly resolved to embroider him a fine waistcoat and the idea gave her great pleasure.

Raising her head she saw that he was offering her the

second package. She opened it and found a necklace of pearls, the largest and most lustrous she had ever seen set in gold to form a pendant.

'It is *purchased*, Joanna,' Kester said quickly. 'It has never been any part of booty. My mother owned one just like it and I would have given that to you had it not long ago been stolen.'

He had been talking as if he could not halt to face a silence, but when Joanna lifted her head to reveal her eyes shining with tears his voice trailed away. 'It is beautiful,' she breathed, 'and you honour me with the thought.'

He took the necklace and fastened it around her slender neck, bringing her a small hand mirror. She looked at her reflection. Her lips were parted, her cheeks flushed and the gems took on the glow of her satin skin.

She put down the mirror carefully and turned to him, willing him to desire her, trying to tell him with her eyes how much she cared for him.

He looked unexpectedly uncertain and touched the pendant between her breasts with tentative fingers. 'Pray, accept the necklace as my Christmas gift. The campaign obliterated the usual festivities, but you made no complaint.'

She was hesitant, wondering if the gifts were simply a conventional expression of the festival. She sought for the right response. 'I have nothing for you, Kester.'

He moved his hands impatiently. 'Why should you have? You have no money. I have been remiss in not making over an allowance to you.'

Too anxious in the light of a possible reconciliation she blundered, 'Oh, no, you must not think I grumble. In our church we do not celebrate Christmas, except in prayer.'

She had torn the fragile cobweb of harmony and his face took on the haughtiness she dreaded. '*My* family did not scorn to celebrate Christmas in a merry way, but of course, Puritans abhor the pleasures of the flesh!'

His dark eyes raked her. 'But not all Puritans follow strict precepts, eh, Joanna? Not all Puritan ladies reject the hotter passions.'

Joanna's face flamed, then paled. She walked away swiftly and entered the smaller chamber where water and towels had been left, and cleansed herself, pulling on a bedgown of white lawn trimmed with pale yellow satin ribbons. When she returned to their bedchamber she had half expected he would have gone, but he was there, staring at the men who still laboured in the light of flambeaux.

The bed was narrower than the one on board ship and it was impossible not to lie together, his lean body forced against hers in a proximity which could have been very sweet. She wondered why he troubled to stay with her when Claris was near and certainly prepared to give him all he wanted. Perhaps she would soon regain her place on the *Lady Margaret*. Joanna felt that she could not much longer endure this mockery of a marriage. She stirred restlessly and Kester groaned softly, placing his hand on her waist from where it moved to her thigh. His breathing quickened and hope sprang in her. She waited for the words of passion and regret, but he pulled her round to face him and took her with a shocking, swift, savagery, leaving her too outraged for tears.

He left the next morning with the others in a flotilla of canoes and boats which were to carry them up river as far as possible before they took to the jungle on their way to Panama. Joanna stood by Major Norman's side watching until they disappeared in the green gloom of the forest, then she sped to her bedchamber where she allowed her tears to fall.

She joined the commander for luncheon, but could eat little and he tried to reassure her. 'Captain Morgan is a brilliant strategist, especially on land. He has victories to his credit which folk believed impossible.'

And many deaths and maimings also, thought Joanna. She retired to her own quarters needing solitude. There was a sound of hammering outside the window and she saw that a scaffolding was being erected to repair a breach in the wall below. She called at a knock at the door and was astonished when Will entered.

'Why have you not gone with your master? You are the only man he can truly rely on.'

Will looked grim. 'That's what I told him, mistress, when he ordered me to stay behind, but there was no arguing with him. I was actually in the boat and he said he felt you needed more protection. I'm to guard you.'

'Go after him, Will. He cannot be left without you. I have had a bad feeling about Panama . . .'

'Seems you both think alike. He's got this idea that you could be in danger. I wondered myself, mistress, with Claris at large.'

'I shall be safe here,' she argued urgently. 'How can she get into the fortress? Could you catch up with him?'

'Oh, aye, easily enough. They're going to travel nigh on forty miles up river and the water's low. They've taken sloops for the artillery and they'll need to negotiate the sandbanks, but I'd not dare disobey the Raven's orders. He says to watch over you and so I will.'

Joanna looked at Will's set face and sighed as she sat down and tried to concentrate on her embroidery. She could not keep her mind on it and after several misplaced stitches she set the work aside. Exhausted by sleeplessness and emotion she leaned back in her chair, resting her head on the high back and closing her eyes. Sounds from outside, the calls of the men, the shriek of seabirds began to blend as she half dozed.

She dreamed of Kester in the first week of their marriage and a smile curved her lips. Through the mists of sleep came a sound of scuffling, then sleep was banished by a yell. She opened her eyes to see Will in the doorway, his mouth still open from his frenzied cry of warning. He launched himself at her and she shrank back, wondering if he had run mad, then he gave a grunt and began to slide to the floor. From his back protruded the handle of a throwing knife.

Joanna saw that Claris was framed in the window. She looked appalled when she realised that she had hit Will.

'Damn you, Puritan,' she screamed, springing down into the room.

Joanna placed herself between Will and the infuriated Claris, but Will said in calm tones, 'Stand aside, mistress. I am armed.'

Joanna saw that he held a small deadly-looking pistol and she knelt by him as he leaned on one elbow, pallor spreading over his face.

Claris looked from one to the other, her expression alternating between her vicious hatred of Joanna and dismayed regret at what she had done to her old shipmate.

'Why did you take my man from me?' she rasped.

'Get out,' ordered Will. 'Go now before I shoot. I don't want to, but if you attempt to hurt Lady Venn . . .'

'Lady Venn!' The words were a wail and Claris's brown eyes were hot with loathing. 'I would have given my soul for him! How could he want a woman like you? Well, you'll not have him back!'

Malignant triumph made her face ugly and Joanna felt sick with sudden fear. 'What have you done?' she cried.

'Yes, what do you mean?' demanded Will in weaker tones.

'If I can't have the Raven no one shall! He'll not return from Panama!'

'Is that all,' said Will scornfully. 'He's too used to danger to fall easily. She's trying to frighten you, Lady Venn.'

Claris's face went red. 'This time he'll not come back. Captain Pryce is going to be revenged for all the insults put upon him. He's taken a vow over an axe!'

Will's breathing rasped through the room and he uttered choked protests.

Joanna cried: 'Is that what you call love? You have let him go without a warning? What kind of love is that?'

'More of the sort he's used to,' shrieked Claris, flinging back her head. 'The kind you'll never be able to give him, Puritan.'

Claris took a step towards Joanna and Will lifted the gun. 'Out,' he gasped, 'before I forget I was once a good Christian Englishman and kill a woman. Out, you vile creature!'

With a curse Claris turned and sprang for the window and in a moment was gone.

Joanna sank to her knees beside Will. 'Oh, Will, you saved my life. Pray God the price will not be your own.'

She sped to find a surgeon who was too old to accompany the expedition, but was skilled. He extracted the knife and bound the wound with healing medicaments.

He warned: 'He's not young, but he's healthy and full of spirit. He could survive and he's got a fixed notion that he must be here to hand you back to your husband when he returns.'

If he returns, mourned Joanna, but she sat by Will's bed as patiently as she could, waiting for him to recover from his deep swoon. Her thoughts kept going to Kester out in the jungle. Even now the vile Captain Pryce might be stalking him, ready to plunge a knife into him, or send a bullet winging to his heart. The man must be deranged from want of revenge for Kester's men would surely hang him or worse if he killed their master.

But that would not bring him back to life and when Major Norman came to see the wounded man she whispered to him of her fears.

He was bluff as he reassured her. 'Sir Christopher has lived with peril for so long it is second nature to him to watch out for himself. And he knows of Pryce's hatred and villainy.'

'It goes far deeper than hatred and villainy,' protested Joanna. 'Pryce has sworn the buccaneer's oath over an axe that he will destroy Sir Christopher.'

She saw by Major Norman's placating smile that he took her for a panicking female. 'An ill-conceived piece of play-acting,' he said indulgently.

Joanna could not give up. 'Even if you do not entirely comprehend, will you send a messenger after my husband to warn him of what has occurred?'

Major Norman shook his head. 'My orders are clear, Lady Venn. Captain Morgan left me with barely sufficient men to complete the repairs and defend the fortress against possible attack. What a fearful thing it would be for our men to return from the expedition to find San Lorenzo in the hands of the enemy.'

'One man only,' begged Joanna.

Again he shook his head, his smile beginning to grow a little fixed and Joanna sank down beside Will, praying for him to awaken so that he might explain.

But when Will did open his eyes the major took no heed of him, obviously putting down his anxiety to the excessive zeal felt by an old retainer for his beloved master.

The surgeon pronounced Will to be a fortunate man. 'The knife has missed his lung and with time and rest he will recover,' he said.

Joanna and Will were left to contemplate the idea of the man they both revered at the mercy of an enemy mad with vengeful fury.

'He *must* be warned,' said Joanna.

Will nodded. 'Find a messenger, mistress. Someone you can trust, even if you have to give him your jewels to ensure his loyalty.'

Joanna's mind scrabbled round like a trapped animal until she came to the conclusion that the only one she could trust enough, save Will, was herself. Lovejoy was horrified, then tearful, as she begged to be allowed to come along.

Joanna was impatient. It was going to be difficult enough to confront Kester with her disobedience without dragging another woman into it.

'You must stay with Will,' she said cajolingly. 'I cannot bear to leave him, but he will understand, and he needs good nursing.'

Thus appealed to the little slave girl applied herself to finding suitable clothes for her mistress and searching for a guide. She knew her way about the fortress and could make herself understood in the local patois and in a short time was able to tell her mistress that she had engaged an Indian with a canoe.

Now Joanna needed gold to pay him and she searched through Kester's possessions, coming upon a small carved box lying unlocked. It contained a letter which bore the instruction that his wife should open it in the event of his death. A *frisson* of terror washed over her as she wondered how deeply he shared her premonition. Almost incoherent in thought she tore open the wafer. The message was short. It thanked her for the happiness she had given him and left her all his worldly goods. The paper had been rudely torn at the bottom and gave no hint of love.

But she could not stop to weep. She found gold and Lovejoy brought the Indian to her. The girl talked to him with some difficulty and Joanna saw that a language barrier would be yet another problem. She and Lovejoy devised a plan whereby the Indian would return with a sign when he had taken his passenger to the boat carrying Sir Christopher Venn. If Joanna returned with him he would be paid by her in person, but only when he had completed his task. Joanna tucked a small wooden cross into her bodice to use as a token.

She took clothes purloined by Lovejoy and pulled on

wide canvas breeches, a calico shirt and brown leather waistcoat, coarse stockings and heavy leather boots stuffed with cotton waste to make them fit. Lovejoy plaited her hair and coiled it round her head and Joanna covered it with a scarf.

Clouds half hid the moon as she climbed fearfully down the scaffolding outside her window, knowing that Major Norman would detain her by any means. When she reached the ground she was wet with perspiration. The Indian led her to the wide river mouth where he had hidden his canoe in the lush vegetation.

A chorus of bullfrogs filled the night with raucous sound, crickets beat their monotonous rhythm, and there was an unearthly shriek from the heart of the jungle as the canoe slid out into open water.

CHAPTER
ELEVEN

As they travelled up river into the rain forest the damp
heat closed in on them and Joanna gasped for air. Within
seconds her shirt stuck to her and the movements
needed to balance in the frail canoe chafed her delicate
skin on the coarse shirt and breeches.

But only her determination to reach Kester mattered
and her feeling of impending disaster grew with every
mile.

The Indian, his face impassive and unreadable,
seemed tireless as his paddle dipped into the water.
Joanna crouched in the bottom of the canoe, desperately
weary. Conditions precluded sleep, but her mind began
to drift in and out of formless dreams, until she was
jerked to horrific wakefulness by a nightmare in which
she saw a man lying motionless with a dagger sticking
from his back. She turned him over to see his face
dissolve from Will's to Kester's.

Her nerves were scarred by terror, added to by the
unidentifiable noises of the forest where unearthly cries
spoke of hunter and hunted.

The sun was rising and steam surrounded them in a
hot miasma as they came upon the rear of the flotilla. As
the Indian paddled past the slower, heavily laden craft
she could hear the mutters of discontent from men who
suffered from their cramped condition and the attacks of
the vicious insects. Joanna stared about her, bewildered.
All her energy had been directed into reaching here and
she had not considered it might be difficult to locate her
husband.

Yet when she saw him she wondered how she could

have doubted that he would stand out above all others
for her. He was in a sloop, his keen eyes raking the river
ahead for shoals and sandbanks and Joanna's guide
brought his canoe alongside. Joanna lowered her tone as
deeply as possible and called out that she had a message
for Captain Venn.

She was about to climb the ladder when her guide
touched her arm and held out his hand. He wanted the
token, but she shook her head smiling. He touched her
arm again, this time not so gently, and thrust his hand
towards her. She tried by signs to make him understand
that she might return, but he grew angry and shook her
arm. The last thing she wanted was an altercation here in
front of Kester's men and before he even knew she was
present, so she handed the wooden token to the Indian,
attempting by signs to tell him he must wait.

Kester watched her walk across the deck and she saw
by his frown and the cold expression in his eyes that she
had not for a moment deceived him. When she would
have spoken he motioned her to silence and directed a
crewman to take the watch before he led her to a tiny
cabin.

Inside he faced her, towering over her, reminding her
that she had resented his invasion of her privacy once;
but now they were married and surely he should not
treat her as a despised interloper.

He kept his voice low: 'How dare you, madam! I
ordered you to remain in the fortress!'

She was hot, exhausted and thirsty and she flared,
'Orders! Always orders! I am not a slave now; I am your
lawful wife.'

His hand shot out to grasp her wrist cruelly. 'Yes, you
are my wife and even more subject to my commands
which, in this case, were given for particularly good
reasons.'

She tried, and failed, to shake herself free, and stared
down at his knuckles, white against her bruising flesh,

and struggled with tears of pain and indignation.

Kester's words came through his teeth. 'Good God, woman, you know that Morgan has forbidden any women on this expedition.'

She tossed her head. 'I cannot imagine why!' The scarf slipped loose and fell to the deck. 'I had no trouble in following you this far.'

'Did you not?' His voice was brittle with sardonic amusement. 'This is only the preliminary stage. We shall arrive at a point where the river is unnavigable over rapids and shoals. That is when the hardships begin.'

Joanna licked her lips. This interview was not what she had come for. 'Kester, I did not disobey you out of trivial considerations. I have a good reason.'

His dark eyes flickered over her, taking in her coronet of hair, the perspiration beading her upper lip, the shirt which clung wetly to her feminine curves, outlining the beauty of her body. He released her wrist and she massaged the purple marks left by his fingers.

'Are you thirsty?' he asked.

She nodded, but when he offered her rum and lemon juice she begged for water.

His laugh barely reached his eyes. 'Would you drink from the river? I fear it is this or nothing.'

Joanna sipped, spluttering at the fiery drink, glancing up into her husband's frowning face.

'Now, madam, tell me the reason you offer for your blatant disregard of my instructions.'

She swallowed hard. 'Kester, I have distressing news for you. Will is lying at the fortress wounded.' She hurried on at his quick intake of breath, explaining rapidly what had happened. 'He is out of danger, the surgeon assured me, and will recover with rest and good nursing. The surgeon and Lovejoy are caring for him.'

'But not you! You decided to leave him!'

'I had no choice,' she said quietly. 'I tried my best to persuade Major Norman to send a message to you. He refused. Kester, please do not be angry with me. I . . . could not bear to think of you in such dreadful peril.'

'So you followed me, against my command. Fighting is my way of life. It was chosen for me and I have pursued it successfully long before I met you.'

'But now I am part of your life and concerned for your safety.'

'I am obliged to you.' His voice was caustic. 'Think you I shall be safer with you to guard me?'

'You are pleased to mock me, but I thought you should know that Captain Pryce has sworn over an axe that you will not leave the jungle alive. I know what such a vow means.'

There was silence and she ventured to look into his face. He was frowning, his eyes fixed on her, dark and watchful. 'Did Claris tell you this?'

When she nodded he asked, 'Have you considered that she was only trying to distress you further?'

'No! She was mad with rage and . . . jealousy . . . she spoke the truth! She wanted me to know that you were in danger of imminent death.'

The words fell between them and Kester said, 'I have been in such danger many times, yet—I have had an odd feeling about Panama . . .'

'Oh, Kester, so have I!'

He looked surprised. 'Have you, indeed?' He touched her hot face with a gentle finger. 'And you thought enough of my welfare to undertake such an uncomfortable journey to warn me!'

She held her breath. Even here she would forget all discomfort if only he spoke the words of love she ached to hear, but he became brisk. 'You must return. I will accompany you until we reach the end of the flotilla, but no further. My post is with my men.'

He strode out shouting in the Indian patois, to return moments later, cursing. 'Your damned guide has left you. Did you reward him before you came aboard?'

Joanna explained, but he cut her short. 'You cannot come with me—yet I cannot send you back. There are no canoes to spare—they are overcrowded already—and no one I could trust sufficiently. They are crazed with lust for Panama's gold and would slit your throat and drop your body in the river so that they could rejoin us.'

'Then—you will take me with you?' She had difficulty in keeping the excitement from her voice.

He caught it and his mouth twisted a little. 'Joanna, how little you comprehend what lies ahead. If there were any way I could spare you . . .'

She washed down a meal of salt meat and hard biscuit with rum and fruit juice after which, too exhausted to notice discomfort, lulled by the effect of strong spirit, she sank on to a hard bunk and lost herself in the oblivion of sleep. Before she drifted off she vowed that Kester would never have cause to curse her disobedience, or be distracted by anxiety for her powers of endurance.

She had many occasions in the days ahead to renew her vow with grim determination, sitting in the sloop, a target for myriads of mosquitoes which fastened on her sweet young flesh, her stomach rebelling against the hard tack and limited drink, her ears assailed by the curses and moans of the men who paddled and heaved the canoes up river over the ever increasing shoals and sandbanks. Kester had no time to waste in reproaches and she stayed in the hot little cabin out of sight.

When her husband took brief periods of rest she vacated the bunk and sat on the deck, watching as he slept. He had explained that the plan was to force a passage as far as Venta de Cruce from which it was believed to be only a day's march to Panama.

'It will be safe to leave you there with an officer and the men who are to guard the boats, Joanna. I shall return for you quite quickly.'

But the river was unusually low and eventually the army had to abandon their vessels and strike through the forest, following the river course.

Kester was worried. 'No one has any real idea how long the journey will take now. I dare not leave you behind. The men are like children who cannot see more than a day or two ahead. You would not be safe.'

Joanna looked at the bank where vegetation proliferated in an apparently impenetrable wall of green. Kester followed her gaze. 'It is not so bad in much of the forest,' he said drily.

He was right. After a way had been hacked through Joanna found herself in a place of savage beauty. Trees with trunks like cathedral columns rose high above them holding up a canopy of leaves and branches which excluded all light but an eerie green gloom. The forest floor was a carpet of leaves and lianas hung down in pale wreaths. Voices echoed as if they were indeed in a mighty church.

Joanna took her place in the long column of marchers and said quietly, 'I thought you said the jungle was fraught with hardships. It is not so at all.'

His answering smile was grim. 'We have scarce begun.'

He was right and Joanna had to hang desperately to her resolve not to whine. There were places where the jungle closed in on them in a tangled mass, sudden terrifying swamps into which they floundered. She learned to know hunger. Not the pleasant emptiness experienced after a brisk walk in winter, or a stroll through English summer fields, but a gnawing, torturing pain which invaded her body by day and infiltrated her sleep at night.

Kester tried as much as he could to ease the hardships for her, but he could not produce food where there was none to be had, nor temper the harsh climate to suit the English rose.

One night they sat at the foot of a tree beneath a rough shelter of boughs and he held her close to his side with an arm still vitally strong. She leaned her head on his shoulder. 'Is there never a breath of clean air here? No coolness of spring or winter?'

'There are no seasons as we know them. Each tree seems to drop its leaves in some rhythm of its own.'

She sighed and he looked down at her. She had pulled off her hat. Her gold hair was dark-streaked with sweat. She looked up into his face, rough with several days growth of beard and wondered if her own eyes were as haunted with hunger and fatigue as his.

He was about to speak, but an altercation brought him to his feet. Quarrels among the desperate men were becoming more frequent and the commanders were forced to use all their strength and guile to prevent a rebellion.

He rejoined her. 'If we do not find food soon we shall have a mutiny.'

On the fifth day the situation was relieved when they discovered sacks of meal and jars of wine and plantains hidden beneath rocks by fleeing Spanish settlers. Joanna thought that nothing had ever tasted so good as the small cakes cooked roughly over stones.

They lay the sixth night by a river, Joanna curled in the curve of her husband's arm. The hardships they shared had engendered a certain comradeship which she found sweet. The air here was fresher and blew softly upon her face and she had almost become inured to the perpetually soggy forest floor and the dripping lianas which brushed their faces.

Her presence had inevitably been discovered by Henry Morgan who had raged at Kester then forgotten it. He had far too many problems to bother about a woman who was unlikely to survive the expedition anyway.

At last, on the ninth day they ascended a mountain

and Joanna leaned against Kester, looking down disbelievingly at the waters of the South Seas.

'We've done it,' exulted Kester. 'We have crossed the Isthmus—twenty-four miles of uncharted forest. I would not have believed it possible that a gently reared woman could have displayed such courage and endurance. You truly are a fitting wife for a privateer.'

His beard was thick and dark, his eyes rimmed with weary shadows, but his commendation filled her with joy. If she could not win his love she would continue to deserve his pride. She could not feel regret at having followed him.

From here they could also see the city of Panama. Joanna stared down at the roofs and spires and the sense of impending danger flooded back. They had caught glimpses of Captain Pryce, but he had taken care to keep away from them. Yet his eyes expressed his relentless hatred and Joanna feared him.

The buccaneers forgot the jungle with all its grim horrors; put aside remembrance of companions who had died from snake bite or fever, Indian arrows or alligators, and swarmed down the hill towards the herds of cattle which grazed before the city.

Joanna ate beef only half cooked and felt strength beginning to return.

Kester was reluctant to leave her. 'I must go, Joanna,' he said. 'Stay on the hill out of sight.' He handed her a small pistol. 'Never allow yourself to fall prisoner. By the time the men have completed their work our enemies will think only of dreadful revenge if they take prisoners.'

She nodded, too choked to speak and watched him stride down the hill with his men until his lithe form was lost to view in the heavy growth at the base. He took her heart with him.

She could see clearly the marshy plain before Panama and she watched through the long, hot hours, loathing the sights, yet unable to take her eyes from the place where her husband was fighting. Two squadrons of Spanish cavalry and four regiments of foot drove a thousand wild bulls before them, but their plan to deflect the legendary ferocity of the buccaneers rebounded on them as the bulls, wounded and terrified, turned back on their owners, scattering and trampling horses and men. The Spaniards rallied, but they were defeated.

Joanna waited, praying, and when she saw Kester climbing the hill she ran to him, tears of relief streaming down her face. His head was bound by a blood-stained cloth and another was twisted round his arm.

He threw himself on the grass and she knelt by him, searching his face with eyes large with privation. 'The battle is over,' he confirmed. 'Hundreds of Spaniards are dead, though only a handful of our men.' He sighed. 'Now the real carnage will begin.'

Joanna sat back on her heels. 'I thought you would be used to it.'

He threw her a dark look. 'Well, I am not. I fight as a patriot, but slaughter and torture of victims is not for me.'

'Then stay with me. If you hate it so much you are better here.'

His grin was twisted. 'You make it sound simple, but my place is down there. The men are half mad. After the deprivations they are like ravening beasts. I have no stomach for it, but maybe I can deflect their revenge from some poor creatures.'

He washed the grime of battle from himself with clear spring water and permitted her to wring out his bandages and replace them, gritting her teeth at the sight of deep gashes.

Then he led her to the harbour where several captured ships floated at anchor. She was installed in the cabin of one of the best and at last was able to strip and clean herself properly. She had grown thin and her flesh was pierced by many scratches and insect bites. Robert Jennison, who was aboard to tend wounded men, gave her lotion to ease and heal her.

Smoke drifted constantly over the harbour, bearing anguished screams from the burning city and he groaned, rubbing red-rimmed eyes. 'God, but these buccaneers are bloodthirsty ruffians. I'm glad my work keeps me here.'

The carnage lasted until the once lovely city was a charred ruin in which whole families had perished. Kester came to see her when he could, saying little, lying with her in the box bed, taking his solace in her body which she gave willingly, sensing he needed escape from horror.

After three weeks he told her to prepare herself and she mounted a mule in a long column which moved once more into the jungle. One hundred and seventy-five beasts were laden with bales containing rich silks, gold and silver, and priceless gems. The men, well fed and refreshed, strode along well pleased with their work while slaves stumbled hopelessly beside them.

They made camp the first night in a ruined ambuscade and Kester comandeered a small hut where they could be alone. Joanna was thankful to be under cover. After the comparative comfort of the vessel she found the jungle even more oppressive, though she was grateful to be riding a mule.

Kester dragged a black fur from a bale and spread it over a wooden bed while Joanna kneaded flour and herbs into a dough. The resultant fare, eaten with strips of salt meat, was spartan.

'As soon as you have cleared up you must rest,' he said. 'The journey back will be easier, but still grim.'

'What of you?' She felt she could not rest without seeing he was safe.

'I shall join you, but first I must talk to the other captains.'

When he had gone she washed the pans, almost amused at the idea of domesticity in such incongruous circumstances, then she poured fresh water and cleaned herself. She decided to await Kester's return before retiring and pulled on the soft breeches and shirt he had procured for her in Panama. The sight of them recalled those terrible days and she heard in memory the terrible shrieks and smelled the acrid smoke. The sense of dread which had never quite left her returned to plague her. She tried to shake it off. Kester had survived Panama. Captain Pryce was still alive, she knew, but surely even his blood lust was satisfied by now.

Then, without any room for doubt, she knew that Kester was in danger. She snatched up her pistol and flew outside. She walked towards the huts where Morgan and the other captains were, creeping cautiously past those where men played noisy games of chance, gambling away their share of the booty which awaited them, or sported with women of the town who had followed them from Panama.

A drunk reeled past her and she shrank into the shadows. He lurched down the dirt street and she hurried on. A door opened and she saw Kester clearly outlined in the flickering lamplight. She could never mistake his form. She began to move to him, scarcely knowing what she would say to him. Then she saw that someone else had been watching. A man who stepped from the shadow of a hut just in front of her within touching distance of Kester. Her heart seemed to stop beating and her tongue clove to the roof of her mouth. She waited. Her tired brain might be distorting events. The man could be a guard, or even a friend who waited to talk. Kester moved into the shadows and the man melted from view. Kester was almost level with her and she began to believe she had allowed herself to become over fearful. She was about to step into the moonlight which was beginning to cast a blue glow over the am-

buscade when the man stepped out behind her husband.
He raised his arm and she saw a gleam of metal.

Almost lulled she was held transfixed by surprise and
dread and although it could have been only seconds
before she recovered it seemed like leaden hours.

'Kester, beware!' she screamed.

Kester, his instincts as alert as a tiger's, ducked as the
man fired. There was a brilliant flash of fire, a loud
report, and a cry. Kester fell and as Joanna darted to him
she saw that his assailant was lifting a second pistol to his
head.

She aimed her own straight at the assassin and fired
and he fell like a stone and did not move.

Joanna dropped to her knees by Kester who groaned.
'You're alive,' she sobbed, shielding him with her arms,
tears raining down on him.

'Thanks to you,' he said, 'though I've been hit. Now
dry your eyes or I'm like to drown.'

The track was filled with men and Kester was carried
to his own hut. Joanna looked down at the still mound at
her feet. Someone turned it over and she recognised
Captain Pryce's face, rigid in death.

Shuddering racked her body. Deliberately she had
lifted her hand and killed a fellow being. She turned and
stumbled after her husband, wondering how she could
ever obtain forgiveness when she knew in her heart that
faced by the same situation she would do exactly the
same thing again. Her love for her husband outweighed
all other emotion.

Love, passion, death, revenge; all seemed to link in
her mind like a hideous chain and at last she understood
how the gentle young man had been turned into a vengeful demon by the murder of his loved ones and his own
subsequent torture. If she could have turned back time
she would have behaved so differently towards him.
When he asked to meet her father she should have
expressed gratitude that a royalist was eager to place

himself for judgment before a Puritan. If she had begun to spin a tenuous thread of love in Kester's heart she must have snapped it by her priggish reaction.

Now he was wounded, perhaps gravely. And even if the assassin's ball was not responsible for killing him she could not see how he was to be got out of this damned jungle. And her recognition of the way she had failed him might have come too late.

CHAPTER
TWELVE

SHE entered the hut. Kester was lying on the bed and
Robert Jennison, who had cut away his shirt, was
probing the wound with expert fingers. When Kester saw
his wife he smothered a groan.

Jennison turned, 'This is no place for a woman.'

Joanna looked at Kester's ashen face, his eyes pain
filled above his beard; she saw how much blood he was
losing. Surely it flowed too copiously for recovery.
Every instinct cried out that she should stay and offer to
help, but there were others present and she knew that
she could faint and become a hindrance.

So she staggered out and leaned on the hut, her
stomach heaving, and looking up at the brilliant star-
filled sky she prayed. That same sky was above the *Lady
Margaret* where she lay at anchor by San Lorenzo.
Would she and Kester ever pace her decks again, or lie
together in the sumptuous cabin?

She covered her ears to deaden a stifled cry of agony
from the hut, and at last Jennison came to fetch her.

'He'll live,' he assured her. 'He's survived worse than
this.'

Kester slept fitfully and she watched him, rising when
he called for a drink. He made no complaint, but the
morning found him very pale and when he tried to sit
astride a horse he collapsed from loss of blood. Joanna
took charge, ordering men to fashion a litter between
two mules. Kester grumbled at such feminine fussiness,
but he allowed himself to be helped into the litter. His
own men obeyed all her instructions and she saw that
they regarded her with new respect.

She assumed them to admire her stoicism until Kester explained that now she had killed Pryce she was considered to be a worthy member of the band of brothers. Far from feeling flattered she felt sick, recalling again and again the dead face of the evil Pryce as his sightless eyes were fixed heavenwards, and the often repeated commandment against murder rang in her head.

Then she had no chance to think of anything but trying to save Kester from the worst tribulations of the journey as the pack animals sweated and heaved their way along the uneven forest trail, sinking into swamps which sucked at their bellies, whinnying at the attacking hordes of insects, balking stupidly at every obstacle. Joanna strained at the bridle of the leading mule which shared Kester's litter and cajoled and cursed in turn. By the time the ragged army reached a navigable tributary of the river Kester was too ill to swallow anything but fruit juice.

Morgan made camp by the small stream to await the arrival of ransom for his wealthier captives and two men paddled Joanna and her husband along the narrow weed-choked waterway in a constant streaming damp in which no wound had any chance to heal. He was at last lifted in the sloop and the last lap of the nightmare voyage began, Joanna marvelling at her ability to survive so long without rest.

In the fortress Kester was borne to their room where a horrified Lovejoy prepared lotions for their stings and scratches and a barber shaved Kester's beard.

Joanna stripped her husband's body and washed it with warm water and soft rags, massaging the skin with oil and as she touched him with gentle tenderness he watched her with eyes sunk beneath dark brows.

Major Norman was full of apologies at having allowed Lady Venn to embark on so madcap an adventure.

Kester's white lips twisted in a grin. 'A determined female is impossible to control, sir, and to tell the truth it is lucky for me she followed, for undoubtedly she saved my life.'

Joanna held her breath waiting for him to tell the major she had destroyed Pryce, but Kester's eyes met hers understandingly and he said no more, allowing the major to believe he had been referring to her good nursing.

Will Buckley staggered in, still a little weak from his own wound, but joyful at seeing his master, and the two men greeted one another. .

'Any news of Claris?' asked Kester.

Will shook his head. 'She's holed up somewhere. The major sent out search parties, but she'll be too cunning for them.'

Kester gave a small grin which Will returned. Joanna realised that they were glad that Claris had not been taken and felt a quick surge of indignation. After all, she had tried to murder her. Then her new awareness came to her aid and she realised that she too hoped that Claris would escape. It seemed that in spite of herself she felt a bond with the buccaneers.

Kester's great strength reasserted itself and his health began to return. Now the danger was over Joanna waited for a sign which proved he loved her, but she was bitterly disappointed. She went on tending him with meticulous care or sat in their room quietly sewing.

One day he said suddenly, 'It is time we moved on. We cannot remain here for ever. Are you ready to leave?'

Her jangled nerves leapt and she was flooded with irritation. 'To go back to privateering, I suppose you mean!'

'You are my wife. You must go where I go.'

'I see! As usual I am given no choice.'

She expected his anger and was surprised when he said quietly, 'You have never considered there is much difference between my own brand of privateering and the piracy of Pryce, have you?'

She dropped her sewing and glared at him, her hands clenched. 'That . . . that is an insult to me. I abhorred Pryce, but you . . .'

'Yes, Joanna?'

His voice was soft, but she could not meet his eyes, unable to endure the mockery she would find in them. 'You—are—different. You—are my husband!'

The words were stilted and she regretted them instantly. Why had she not the courage to proclaim her love. Love might engender love. She glanced up at him to find him regarding her steadily. She tried to gather up some shreds of valour, but he spoke first.

'Why did you follow me to Panama?'

She was astonished. 'You already know the answer! I had to warn you of Pryce's threat.' She picked up her sewing and made spurious attempts at setting in a stitch.

'If he had killed me you would have been a wealthy widow. And you know it, for you read my letter.'

Her face coloured hotly as he continued: 'You could have married a Puritan gentleman of your own choosing.'

It is you my heart has chosen, she cried inwardly, but his voice had been cruelly derisive and she remained silent.

His tone was cool. 'You do not speak, madam!'

She said as calmly as her shaking nerves would allow, 'A wealthy widow is welcome in any society, sir.'

'Prim and proper Joanna', he jeered. 'Come here!'

She continued to sit and he threw back the blankets and swung his legs to the floor.

She jumped up and ran to him. 'Kester, you are supposed to rest the wound. It may break out again . . .'

'Then sit by me.' He patted the quilt.

She obeyed him, holding herself rigidly aloof, but he slid one arm round her waist and his long, clever fingers stroked her hair and face.

Of its own volition her body responded and after a
moment of futile resistance she turned her mouth into
the palm of his hand, then leaned down to kiss his lips.

He gave a small humorous groan. 'Easy, woman, I am
not yet permitted to exercise myself.'

Her laugh was ragged as she rose, putting her hands to
her burning cheeks. Then she fled on the pretext of bringing him a cooling drink.

Major Norman kept them informed of events.
Morgan brought his monstrous army to San Lorenzo
where the share-out was made. After the crown and the
officers had been allotted portions it was announced that
only two hundred pieces of eight remained for each man.
To deflect their fury he distributed great casks of wine
and in the ensuing debauchery he left the harbour with
five ships, taking most of the food supplies with him.
Others, following his example, sailed, and among them
was Claris. The major was indignant when he told them
that she had comandeered Pryce's vessel and crew who
apparently were prepared to serve under so ferocious a
woman. She had actually had the temerity, he told Kester and Joanna, to have an educated crewman write to
him and had also left a letter for them.

They read it together. The man's education must have
been limited but he managed to convey the facts. Claris
considered she had won Pryce's ship in fair contest with
the others and she had decided that it was only just that
Joanna should enjoy her husband after having killed for
him.

Her logic was that of the savage brethren of the coast
and Joanna quailed before it, though she was deeply
relieved to know that Claris had given up her desire for
revenge. She stole a look at Kester, but his face was
almost impassive. A small, appreciative grin flickered
there for a moment and was gone, but it reminded her
that her husband had pursued a life of extreme ruthless-
ness. She felt the gulf between them widen, aware that

she could never participate willingly in such a mode of living.

Kester deemed it wise to remove his household out of the rowdy fortress town and the *Lady Margaret* slipped out of harbour and made for Port Royal. Their arrival was noted and the Modyford's carriage awaited them on the quay. Sir Thomas immediately took Kester into his bookroom while Elizabeth led Joanna into her pretty sitting room overlooking the hills.

She had a worried frown on her gentle face as she said, 'Such trouble, we are in, my dear. It seems that a treaty was formed with Spain and my husband should not have granted commissions to raid Panama. Spain is bitterly angry and demanding retribution.'

Joanna's instant fear was for her husband. Governments had a notoriously short way with those who offended and he had no friends left at court.

After dining with the Modyfords she and Kester left beneath a brilliant moon for their villa in the foothills. As soon as they were alone Joanna expressed her fears.

In the slanting moonlight she saw his grim smile. 'They are not interested in the captains. It is Morgan they want, forgetting that without him the colonists could not survive.'

He sounded bitter and Joanna fell silent. She recalled with painful nostalgia the first time she had made this journey. What joy she had been about to learn and what gnawing regret she suffered now.

It was late and they retired at once and as she lay in the comfort of the fourposter with its intricately carved supports and delicately embroidered hangings she was almost able to convince herself that the past weeks of misery would be wiped out and Kester would become as close as before.

But although he made love to her with exquisite skill, drawing from her the response she could never deny, she waited in vain for a word of love. She lay awake a long

time wondering how she could continue to endure this
twilight marriage with a man who gave everything but
his heart.

The following day they climbed to the sunny little
plateau and Kester stripped and dived into the clear
water. She followed his example, removing all her
clothes for the first time and standing naked, and un-
ashamed, her soft loveliness outlined against the glossy
dark green bushes. The water caressed her skin and
together she and Kester swam to a large flat rock where
they lay in the hot sun, while droplets from the waterfall
showered them.

The sea was clearly visible in the distance, stretching
away to the horizon where it merged with the sky. The
breathtaking beauty seemed to underline personal frustration and Joanna slid back into the pool. Perhaps she
had overestimated her strength or lost her concentration
for she forgot how to swim and found herself thrashing
about, her legs seeking a foothold, panic invading her as
water filled her mouth and nose. Then Kester's strong
arm was around her neck, holding her chin above water
as he guided her to safety.

On shore he helped her on with her shift which clung
damply to the graceful outlines of her flesh. Her hair
streamed down her back and her eyes were dark with
remembered terror.

Kester touched her cheek with a caressing finger.
'You must not try to run before you can walk,' he
murmured. 'Never fear, I will teach you all the
skills.'

All the skills! Including that of making love, she supposed. But she could teach him a greater lesson. That of
giving oneself in the fullest way, involving heart and soul
as well as body. All her pride was slipping from her. She
could not continue in this way. She must tell him of her
true feelings and trust that he was compassionate
enough to use her kindly.

She sank to her knees on the grass, staring up at him, seeking the right words. Then she realised that Kester was looking at her wonderingly. He could not fail to read the message written so clearly in her eyes and he crouched on the grass in front of her.

To her immense gladness she saw that he was responding in the way which had filled her dreams. There was no mistaking the light in his dark eyes.

'Joanna,' he breathed. 'Oh, Joanna, how long have you loved me?'

'I cannot tell when it began,' she answered shakily. 'Perhaps from the beginning.'

His arms went round her. 'And I love you too, my dearest wife. I thought there was no hope for me—that I had forfeited your trust for ever.'

Her answer was to find his eager lips with hers and their kiss held no restraint. It lengthened and he drank in the sweetness of her mouth as if parched from a long drought. They sank on to the soft grass and the world spun crazily as their bodies fused and moved in unison, sending their love winging to the bowl of heaven, swallowing their doubts.

Afterwards they lay side by side looking up into the sky.

Kester said softly, 'To think your love was there and I was too big a coward to ask for it.'

'You! A coward!' she jeered gently.

'You had the power to fill me with terror as no battle ever could.'

He kissed the top of her head and wound a gold tendril of hair about his finger. 'We have been at dreadful odds. Yet the hope of your love was the lifeline to which I clung.'

'When did it begin?'

'I think when you stood on deck that first day and your eyes sparked defiant fire at me. Or was it when you sprang at me like a tigress and tried to scratch me? Such courage I had to admire, though it went against the grain to give a Puritan any virtues.'

She said slowly, 'Yet you bought me in that dreadful slave market in front of all those men, adding to my shame.'

He groaned softly. 'My beloved, what other way was there? If you knew the hell you put me through. I had to guess at where Claris had taken you, then when we arrived in Tortuga and I learned you were already on the slave block . . . For the first time since my family died, I prayed . . . prayed that I would be the one to purchase you. I had not enough men to take you by force on Tortuga.'

'If you had not forced me to sleep aboard the *Lady Margaret* . . .! I thought you cared only for your treasure—or for Claris.'

'You were jealous? So soon after our meeting and after all that had passed between us?'

Joanna flushed. 'I believe I was, though I could not admit it, even to myself.'

Kester grinned, then flicked her cheek with a gentle, admonishing finger. 'Foolish child. I sent you aboard for your own protection. My seadogs could not take their covetous eyes from your beauty. One incident would have set them brawling.'

'I see.' She thought for a moment, then asked in a small voice, 'Why did you make me wear those awful gowns when you captured me? I am sure you had others. They made me look like a . . .'

He stopped her mouth with a kiss. 'My dear wife, do not sully your lips. I tried to remove the honest temptation you were offering me by trying to dress you in a way my mother would have abhorred. Instead, the contrast offered by your clear, innocent face and those tawdry garments only added to your sweet purity.'

He rose and pulled her to her feet. They dressed and he tied the tapes of her shift and gown. Then he took her tortoiseshell comb from her hand and drew it through her silken hair.

As he did so he said gently, 'Joanna, we *must* go to England one day.'

She held her breath. This was a path she must tread warily. He continued, 'We were both partly right about it. We will wait a while and I will write to your father which will give him time to become accustomed to the idea of me as a son. Then—when we go—and you can place a grandchild—or maybe two—in his arms—he will surely forgive us.'

Joanna's face took on a deeper rose and Kester smiled and busied himself with tying her hair back in a silver ribbon.

'Of course,' he said, 'it is false to ask for forgiveness if one is still committing the offence and I have lost the wish to continue the life of a privateer. I am leaving the sea, my love . . .'

She turned quickly, 'Oh, Kester, to give up privateering . . . that is wonderful news, but will you be happy without your ship?'

He said firmly, 'There will be opportunities in plenty for sailing. If I had been honest with myself I would have admitted years ago that my lust for revenge would have been deplored by my good parents. Since I have learned to love you I have viewed life through your eyes. I have seen myself as you—as my mother must have seen me—and I have disgusted myself. The scenes in Panama have completed what you began. Never again shall I be party to such carnage.'

He pulled her close and murmured into her hair, 'Think you I shall prove a worthy husband to my little Puritan?'

She leaned back so that she could see his face and said firmly, 'Kester, I also have been learning. When I killed Captain Pryce . . .' she still could not refer to it without stumbling over the words '. . . I could not feel proper repentance. All I knew was that I was thankful I had saved you. Now I can comprehend how a person can be driven.'

'Generous Joanna. So there are no more secrets between us. Or have you any other questions?'

'One,' she admitted. 'Once you made love to me and then looked at me in disgust . . .'

'I have not forgotten,' he interrupted. 'I was disgusted, but not with you. With myself for bruising your body in anger. But there will be no more forcing, will there?'

She shook her head and he said, staring at the ocean. 'I felt it my duty to send you to your betrothed, though I knew I was destroying my chance of happiness. Then that tardy babe reunited us.' He laughed. 'I vow I shall send it a reward. And I shall shower you with gifts, my love. When I believed I should not return from Panama I left you all I owned, but even then I was less than brave. I wrote a message telling you I loved you, then tore it away.'

'And I might never have known! Oh, why?'

'I felt I deserved only your loathing. I had raped your innocence as surely as if I had taken you as a captive slave. I could not add an unwanted love to your burden.'

She pulled his head down to hers and her kisses told him all he needed to know of love and forgiveness.

At dinner that night Joanna asked Kester what plans he had made for the future. She was content, she told him, to pursue any path he chose.

'I know it,' he responded, 'but I hope you will like what I have decided. Perhaps I always knew in my heart that I would leave the sea. Long ago I bought a plantation on the coast of America and have visited it whenever I could. I have had a good overseer in charge and it has prospered. I have always felt drawn to the life. Would you be content to be the wife of a farmer, Joanna?'

Her shining eyes and delighted smile were answer enough.

'Many of my men are those who have drifted to me through misfortune and would be glad of the opportunity to settle,' said Kester. 'I shall take some of them with me. I owe them all a debt of loyalty and shall make sure that each is rewarded.'

The *Lady Margaret* was fitted out for her voyage and sailed before a favourable wind with a small loyal crew.

Kester and Joanna stood by the rail and watched as the blue mountains sank out of sight. The strong ocean breezes sent the craft skimming through the waves and Kester murmured, 'Farewell Raven . . . .!'

'And welcome to Sir Christopher Venn, gentleman and farmer,' completed Joanna.

She sighed as she remembered the happiness she had found on the island of Jamaica. 'We shall not return, shall we, Kester' she murmured.

'You feel as I do,' he agreed. 'Let the Raven and his past remain buried there for ever.'

He leaned on the rail. 'I knew you would be at one with me, Joanna, and I hope you also understand the last act I performed there. I gave Modyford a warrant to make over the villa to Claris.'

He felt Joanna's swift turn of her head. 'She has never meant anything to me in the way you do, yet I owe her something for her fidelity. One day she may need a haven to escape to.'

Joanna touched his arm. 'I am glad. It proves what I know to be true—that you are a man of honour.'

He drew her to him and they linked arms. Kester took a look round his ship where the sailors were busy at their tasks, then led his wife into their cabin and Will Buckley, sitting on a coil of rope in the sun, looked at the closed door with a grin of pure delight.